Praise for the Unknown Assassin Series

"When James Bond was a little boy, he wanted to grow up to be half as hard-core as Boy Nobody."
—Barry Lyga, *New York Times* bestselling author of *I Hunt Killers*

★ "[A] violent, entertaining twist on the teen spy novel . . . Will keep readers riveted."
—*Publishers Weekly* (starred review)

★ "[*I Am the Weapon*] is like a darker version of Alex Rider [and] Thomas in James Dashner's Maze Runner series."
—*VOYA* (starred review)

"Will leave readers on the edges of their seats . . . Hollywood-esque thrills."
—*Kirkus Reviews*

"[A] highly suspenseful, compulsively readable futuristic thriller . . . Readers will be clamoring for the next volume."
—*Booklist*

"Fast, furious and fun."
—*Kirkus Reviews*

I AM THE TRAITOR

THE UNKNOWN ASSASSIN
BOOK 3

ALLEN ZADOFF

LITTLE, BROWN AND COMPANY

NEW YORK   BOSTON

Copyright © 2015 by Allen Zadoff

All rights reserved. In accordance with the U.S. Copyright Act of 1976, the scanning, uploading,
and electronic sharing of any part of this book without the permission of the publisher is unlawful
piracy and theft of the author's intellectual property. If you would like to use material from the
book (other than for review purposes), prior written permission must be obtained by contacting
the publisher at permissions@hbgusa.com. Thank you for your support of the author's rights.

Little, Brown and Company

Hachette Book Group
1290 Avenue of the Americas, New York, NY 10104
Visit us at lb-teens.com

Little, Brown and Company is a division of Hachette Book Group, Inc.
The Little, Brown name and logo are trademarks of Hachette Book Group, Inc.

The publisher is not responsible for websites (or their content) that are not owned by the publisher.

First Paperback Edition: June 2016
First published in hardcover in June 2015 by Little, Brown and Company

The Library of Congress has cataloged the hardcover edition as follows:

Zadoff, Allen, author.
   I am the traitor / Allen Zadoff. — First edition.
      pages cm. — (The unknown assassin ; book 3)
   Summary: After breaking free of The Program, Boy Nobody is on a mission of his own to
reclaim his life and rescue his friend Howard from the secret organization that has turned him
and other orphaned children into trained assassins—but he has no idea who, if anyone, he can
trust, or what the consequences will be if he succeeds in bringing down The Program.
   ISBN 978-0-316-19972-8 (hardcover) — ISBN 978-0-316-33687-1 (ebook) —
ISBN 978-0-316-33689-5 (library edition ebook) 1. Assassins—Juvenile fiction. 2. Child
soldiers—Juvenile fiction. 3. Brainwashing—Juvenile fiction. 4. Secret societies—Juvenile
fiction. 5. Conduct of life—Juvenile fiction. [1. Assassins—Fiction. 2. Brainwashing—
Fiction. 3. Secret societies—Fiction.] I. Title.
   PZ7.Z21Iap 2015
   [Fic]—dc23

                                                                                    2014040291

Paperback ISBN 978-0-316-19974-2

10 9 8 7 6 5 4 3 2

LSC-C

Printed in the United States of America

For my brother Jeff

THIS USED TO BE MY HOME.

It's an ordinary two-story house on a suburban cul-de-sac about a mile from Brighton High School. There's a bed of flowers in a plot in the front yard. There were different flowers in the same spot five years ago.

The day I left this place. The day I saw my father die, or thought I did.

I was ordered never to return, yet here I am, sitting in a car, watching the house, and remembering a part of my life I've been trained to forget.

Movement behind me. The summer sun glints off the windshield of a Volvo wagon. I can see one occupant, a female, driving toward my car.

I start the car, readying myself for evasive action.

I track the wagon first in the rearview, then in my peripheral, then straight on as it drives past and continues down the road. It does not slow or swerve. There's no indication that the driver is here for any reason having to do with me.

But it is a reminder that I am in danger. Every moment I stay on the street, I risk being detected.

I check the clock on the dash. Three hours until I meet Mike.

I have not come back to my hometown of Rochester, New York, by choice, but out of necessity. This is where Mike wants to meet, where he will tell me what he knows about my friend Howard's disappearance.

Howard was secretly working for me on my last assignment, trying to untangle truth from fiction. I believed Mike killed my father, yet there is evidence to suggest that my father might not be dead.

Before he could tell me what he knew, Howard disappeared.

I've come to find him.

It could be a trap. But I am willing to take that risk, because in my mind, I see the path toward my goal.

Mike. Howard. My father. One leading to the next.

I should go now, but I lean back in my seat and turn off the engine.

I am fascinated by this house and unable to look away. My eyes track up the light green shingles, over to the far right corner window.

That was my bedroom.

A wave of emotion hits me, so intense that it takes my breath away.

I give the feeling a name.

Grief.

I breathe into it. It's better to have no feelings at all, but when they come, I've learned they do not last forever. They arrive in waves, and like waves, they recede. Eventually.

I notice two kids walking down the street toward me, backpacks slung over their shoulders. One is around sixteen, the other thirteen. Similar postures and facial structure.

Brothers.

I glance at the dash clock. Quarter to three. At this time of day, they're probably local kids walking home from summer school.

But they could be Program soldiers disguised as students.

They approach on the opposite side of the street.

I watch. I prepare.

They don't so much as glance at my car. Instead they turn into the cul-de-sac and head for the house. The older kid takes out a key and unlocks the door, then he and his brother go inside, closing the door behind them. I can tell from their behavior that they've done the same thing thousands of times before.

These are not Program soldiers. They are the strangers who live in the house where I grew up.

This used to be my home. Not anymore.

I start the car.

I DRIVE TO THE UNIVERSITY OF ROCHESTER.

My father was a psychology professor here. I walk across campus toward the building where he used to work.

Summer session is in progress, and the campus is mostly quiet, small groups of students walking among the brick and stone buildings along the river. When I was a boy, my father took me to work sometimes, leaving me to read on the leather sofa in his office while he delivered his lectures. Back then the students seemed so much older than me. Now our differences are less about age than purpose.

They lead normal lives. I live the life of a soldier.

The route to the psychology building is ingrained in my muscle memory. I cross the quad, turning left into a three-story redbrick building that houses the psych department and what used to be my father's office.

When I walk in, I see a directory with listings for the philosophy, comp lit, and modern-languages departments. No psychology.

Confused, I head down the hall and tap on the first office door I encounter. A woman in a gray pantsuit looks up from an impressive stack of papers.

"Can I help you?"

"Is this the psych building?" I say.

"Not anymore. They moved about four years ago."

She looks me up and down, trying to figure out why I don't know this information.

"I'm doing a campus tour," I say. "I might apply next year. My dad used to be a professor here."

"So you're a legacy."

"Should be an easy admit, huh?"

"Depends. Does he donate?"

"Every year. With the crappy grades I bring home, he has no choice."

She smiles. "I'm sure you won't have any problems. By the way, where does your dad teach now?"

Time to change the subject.

"Could you tell me where the new psych building is?" I ask.

She spins her chair and gestures out the window behind her, indicating a new structure of steel and green glass in the distance. The building comes to a point like the prow of a ship.

"Thar she blows," the woman says.

"Impressive."

"A large, anonymous bequest. There's an academic center on campus and a research facility downstate in Corning."

Corning. That flags something in my memory. My father took me there years ago.

"That's a lot of resources for a psychology program."

"Lucky them, huh?"

I see the muscles in her jaw clench.

Interdepartment rivalry. I may not have gone to college, but I know the dynamic well enough from The Program. People in an organization tend to compete with one another.

I thank her and turn away before she can ask me any more questions.

"Good luck with your applications," she calls from behind me.

"Thanks," I say as I head out the door. "I'll need it."

I PUSH THROUGH HERMETICALLY SEALED DOUBLE DOORS INTO THE PSYCH BUILDING.

I'm hit by a rush of perfectly cooled sixty-eight-degree air.

I scan the digital directory on the wall near the front entrance until I find the information for Professor Abraham Silberstein, my father's former research partner. His son Joshua was my best friend in elementary school.

I've already looked up Dr. Silberstein's schedule online, so I know he's lecturing today. I use the directory to pull up a map of the building and find the hall on the second floor, then I use the sleeve of my hoodie to wipe my fingerprints off the touch screen.

I take the stairs two at a time, moving like a student late for class. I slip into the rear of a steeply raked, two-hundred-seat lecture hall about half filled with students.

Dr. Silberstein stands in the front of the room, his voice loud through the sound system. He's grown a beard since I last saw him. It's dappled with gray and makes him look older and more distinguished than I remember. PowerPoint slides float by on a video monitor behind him. The term *cognitive dissonance* appears briefly before dissolving in an animated transition.

Silberstein glances up midsentence, his eyes drifting to the back of the hall. He notes me briefly and continues with his lecture, only to glance at me again a second later.

His eyes widen in recognition.

"I'm sorry, that's all we have time for today," he says, abruptly tearing off his microphone and running from the lecture hall.

"Where is he go—" the student nearest me starts to say, but I'm already racing out the back door and down the stairs, arriving just in time to see Dr. Silberstein far ahead of me, pushing his way into the stairwell. I hit the doors and fling myself after him, grabbing the banister for leverage and leaping ten steps at a time.

I catch up to Silberstein at the bottom landing. He's halfway through the basement doors when I reach out and grab the back of his suit jacket.

"Get away from me!" he says, clutching the door frame.

"I just want to talk to you."

"Help!" he shouts.

"Everything okay down there?" I hear a man's voice above me on the staircase, followed by the sound of footsteps.

Silberstein uses the distraction to wriggle out of his suit coat and slip through the door, leaving the coat still in my hands.

A moment later a custodian appears. "I heard shouting," he says.

I can calm the situation down or ratchet it up. Which will help me the most?

"Do you smell that?" I say.

"Smell what?"

"I think it's smoke."

"Oh gosh," he says. "I'd better pull the alarm." He rushes back up the stairs.

I push through the stairway doors, pausing for a moment to check the pockets of Silberstein's suit coat. I find a white magnetic security card in a plastic holder. There's no identifying information on it, so I slip it into my own pocket, ditch the coat, and step into the hallway.

A moment later the fire alarm sounds, a high-pitched, pulsing tone that echoes down the halls.

With the alarm going off, I don't need to worry about drawing attention to myself, so I break into a trot, racing through the basement until I find an exit that lets out on the side of the building.

Silberstein is across the quad, running for all he's worth, sweat evident under the arms of his blue dress shirt. He takes the corner hard, slipping on the grass and almost wiping out before he recovers his balance and disappears behind the building.

I accelerate, dodging a group of students deep in conversation, and I run after him at full speed through the campus, familiar images from my childhood flashing by faster than I can process them.

I race around the corner and see the back of the blue shirt disappearing into a residence hall a few yards away. I slow to a jog, relaxing my posture so I appear to be a student who has forgotten something in his dorm and gone back to retrieve it.

I walk through the front door. There's no security to question me.

I imagine Silberstein's trajectory. He's weaving his way through the building, trying to lose me and looking for an exit that will send him in a new direction.

It's midafternoon, but the dorm is busy, girls crashed in front of TVs in common areas, girls studying with doors open, girls walking back and forth to the bathroom.

Why are there so many girls?

I jump through a group of them sprawled out in the hall, bare legs in shorts forming an obstacle course.

"Is it asshole day?" a girl shouts as I leap over her. That tells me Silberstein was here a minute ago. I move as I think he would move, zigzagging until I find an exit door.

I wedge my shoulder through the door and pop out the rear of the building.

"STOP!" A MAN SHOUTS.

It's a campus police officer. He stands in front of me wearing black slacks and a uniform jacket, a cap pulled low over his forehead. He has the tight build of a trained fighter, unusual for a campus cop.

"Are you a student?" he says.

I decide to play it like an entitled college kid not used to being challenged.

"What the hell else would I be?" I say.

"Since you're coming out of a women's dorm, you could be a lot of things," the cop says. "Pervert tops the list."

A women's dorm? No wonder there were so many girls in there.

I smile, the cat caught with the canary. "I was visiting my girlfriend."

"That's a load of crap," he says.

Impolite language for a campus cop.

The guy grins and pops up the cap to reveal his face.

"Good afternoon, Zach."

It's not a cop. It's Mike.

11

"What are you doing here? We're supposed to meet two hours from now," I say.

"Way ahead of you," he says. "Come to think of it, I'm always ahead of you."

"You followed me?"

"Didn't have to. You're not as unpredictable as you think you are."

I'm trained to be unpredictable in all ways. My movements, my habits, my decisions. Unpredictable and therefore undetectable.

Am I getting sloppy?

"I know why you're here," Mike says.

"It was one of my favorite places in the old days."

He shakes his head. "Let's not bullshit each other."

"Fine. Why don't *you* tell me why I'm here?"

"You want to find your father."

He watches me, seeking a reaction. I don't give him one.

"There are no secrets between brothers," he says.

I glance at his hands. They are relaxed and by his side, seemingly nonthreatening. But you never know with Mike. He could be preparing to strike, and I wouldn't know until the attack was already in motion.

"I guess you've got me all figured out," I say. "What do you want to do about it?"

"Up to you," he says. "Do you feel like grabbing a cup of coffee? Or would you rather fight to the death?"

I know what I'd prefer, but I say, "Coffee sounds good."

MIKE TAKES OFF THE CAMPUS COP JACKET AND HANGS IT ON A METAL FENCE POST.

He slouches his shoulders and in an instant transforms from authority figure to student, almost like an actor getting into character before a performance. I match his energy, and together we head down the stone steps under the Arts Building, where a sign for the Dragon Coffee Shop greets us. "Why don't you grab a seat and I'll get us something at the counter," Mike says, like we're buddies meeting to hang out together.

Mike is relaxed, which only makes me more cautions. I am in danger every moment I'm with him. I must not forget it.

I scope out the coffee shop and I'm hit with a sense of déjà vu. I was in this coffee shop with my father years ago. It had a different name then and different furniture. But there's no question—I was here.

I select a table in the back with a brick wall to one side and the counter behind me. It is the most defensible position in the room.

I turn my chair to the wall and sit sideways so I can watch Mike and the door at the same time.

There are nine students in the room. I map their locations in my head.

I look at Mike waiting in line. The students have no idea that a trained assassin stands inches from them.

A minute later Mike comes over with two coffees and a plate of snacks.

"Oatmeal raisin cookies," he says.

"Did you bake them yourself?"

"Didn't have time. But the sign says they're freshly baked. Do you think we can trust it?"

"I don't think we can trust anything in this place."

Mike grins and puts the plate of cookies in front of me.

"Do you still like oatmeal raisin?" he asks.

Those were my favorite cookies when I was a kid. Mike obviously remembers, and he wants me to know it. Is he trying to bond with me, or is it a test?

"I don't like or dislike anything," I say.

Preference creates patterns and patterns create vulnerability.

"We trained you well," Mike says. "But don't you enjoy a little something every now and again? Secret pleasures? We all have them."

"Do you have them?"

He raises his eyebrows. "I plead the Fifth," he says.

I sip from my coffee, and I wait. Mike brought me here, so it's wise to let him speak first.

Mike pulls out a seat, its metal legs scraping against the floor. He glances from side to side, making sure we can't be overheard.

"Your friend," he says. "The one who disappeared from your hotel room after the last mission."

"Howard."

"Is that his name?"

Howard was working with me in New Hampshire. He risked his life to break into an armed camp and free me. Then he stuck around to search for clues about my real father.

"Do you know who has him?" I ask.

"The Program has him."

I'd thought so. But now I have confirmation.

"They have his laptops, too," Mike says. "That's the bad news. The good news is they can't crack his computer encryptions, so they don't know what he was up to. Yet."

"If they have him, why do they need his computers?"

"That's the interesting part," he says. "He hasn't talked. I guess he's a lot tougher than he looks. Like a geek armadillo or something."

I suppress a smile.

"You're telling me they don't know who he is or what his connection to me is?"

"That's right," Mike says. "So why don't you tell me what your connection is?"

I study Mike's face, trying to determine how much he already knows and how much I can safely give away. I decide to stay as close to the real story as possible.

"He was helping me look for my father."

Mike shakes his head.

"Your father is dead, Zach."

"That's not what you told me in New York," I say.

"What I told you—?"

"In Brooklyn, when you had me restrained in that room. You said my father might be alive."

"No."

I watch Mike's face, trying to detect a lie.

"You were drugged," Mike says. "You heard what you wanted to hear. I'm afraid this has become some sort of an obsession for you."

I think about the moment in Brooklyn. I was waking up after being injected with a knockout drug. Could I have imagined the conversation with Mike?

"How do you know he's dead?" I ask.

"Do I really need to answer that?" Mike says.

"You killed him."

"It wasn't personal, it was my mission. You've done the same thing yourself, taken kids' parents away from them. How many times now?"

"Quite a few."

"It's what we're trained to do," he says. "It's not nice, but it's necessary."

Mike sips at his coffee, peering over the rim of the mug. I imagine grabbing the mug out of his hands and shattering it in his face.

He can sense the danger. He studies me, watching to see whether I'm going to make a move.

"Your anger is misplaced," he says. "It's your father you should be angry at. He's the one who did this to you. Not me, not Mother or The Program. We don't target innocent people."

I've had the same thought myself numerous times. The Program targets people who are guilty. My father did something to bring Mike and The Program into our lives.

"You're probably wondering what he did," Mike says, "but I'm not privy to that information. Not now, and certainly not then. We never learn why. We do our job and we don't ask questions. That's how it's been from the beginning, even before you were in The Program."

"Why are you telling me this now?"

"You're in danger, Zach. You have been in serious trouble these last two missions, but it's nothing compared with this. You're as close to rogue as anyone has ever been. The Program is still a young organization. They haven't dealt with insubordination, and they don't know how to handle it. In my opinion, they have a tendency to overreact. I've done my best to ameliorate the situation. I've championed your cause to Mother and Father. I've advocated for you."

Advocated. Like he's an attorney arguing my defense.

"I appreciate that," I say.

"I don't think you do," Mike says. "Not nearly enough."

I look around the coffee shop. Two students have left. The head count is down to seven plus Mike.

"Your mother and father are dead," Mike says. He waits for me to look up at him. "But you still have a family. If you want us."

I reach for my coffee. I drink it too fast and the hot liquid scalds my throat. The pain helps me to focus.

"Do you want us?" Mike asks.

"I need the truth first," I say.

"I've told you the truth as I know it."

I reach into my pocket and finger the security pass I got from Silberstein's coat. In all this talk, Mike hasn't mentioned the professor. Why did he run away from me? What's going on in the University of Rochester psych department?

Mike knows more than he's saying, but I'll never find out if I attack him now. Better to make him an ally than an enemy.

I lean in and lower my head, taking a submissive position. "What should I do, Mike?"

He looks pleased.

"First of all, this quest of yours has to end. Right now."

I nod, conceding the point.

Mike grins. "Then we move on to the next step," he says. "Cleanup."

"Explain."

"Your friend Howard is in a holding house in upstate New York, a couple hours south of here. As I told you, he's held up through field interrogation," Mike says. "But soon they will move him someplace and ask him questions in a way that will guarantee answers. He will talk. It's just a matter of time and technique."

Mike is right about that. The Program can make anyone talk. Eventually.

"So you have an opportunity," Mike says.

"An opportunity?"

"To kill him."

I sit back in my chair, the breath suddenly gone from my lungs.

This is what Mike wants from me?

"There has to be another way," I say.

He shakes his head. "I know you care about this kid, but right now you're only under suspicion with The Program. Once they break him, you'll be out of options, and I won't be able to help you."

"Why are you helping me now?"

"You don't get it, do you?"

I shake my head.

"I need you, you idiot." Mike leans toward me. "You're all I have."

I've never seen Mike vulnerable like this. I analyze his breathing and facial expressions, and it seems like he's telling the truth.

He says, "You know my family's dead, just like yours. I had to make a decision back then, much like the one I'm asking you to make now."

"You chose to stay with The Program."

"I chose life. I mourned my losses and moved on. I thought you had, too."

"Maybe it's not as easy for me."

Mike's face softens. "Sometimes I forget how young you are, Zach.

I know you feel old because you've seen a lot of death, but you're still just a kid. Here's the deal. If you walk away today, you're committing suicide. If you stay, you give yourself a chance to grow up and gain some perspective on this thing."

"*Gain perspective?* How am I supposed to do that?"

"You accept reality," Mike says. "You lost one family, so you have to find another. The Program is my family now, and I'll do anything to keep us together."

"I'm not like you."

"Not yet," Mike says, "but if you stick around, who knows how you'll feel after a few years?"

I look down at the cookies on the table. I think about the time Mike and I first met. We were best friends for a little over a month before my life changed forever. I trusted him then, and I was burned.

Do I trust him again now?

There are two possibilities that I can see.

One, Mike is being straight with me, and he's giving me a chance to set things right before The Program finds out what I've done.

Two, Mike is lying about my father. By killing Howard, I will destroy my best chance to find out the truth.

I say, "Did Mother send you to make this offer?"

"It's coming from me directly," he says. "Mother knows nothing about it."

Mike crosses his arms, waiting.

"Maybe you're right," I say. "It would be stupid to commit suicide. I need to give this some time."

I glance up to see Mike smiling.

"You made the right choice," he says.

I PRESS DOWN ON THE GAS, AND THE ACCORD RESPONDS WITH A ROAR.

I'm on I-490, heading southeast out of Rochester. Mike's relaxing in the passenger seat, one leg propped up on the dash.

"You and I on a mission together," he says. "It's sort of like the old days."

"In the old days, I didn't have a license," I say.

"It's hard to believe you were only twelve when I met you."

"Is this why you wanted us to meet in Rochester?" I say. "So we could reminisce?"

Mike nods. "I wanted to remind you of where we began. And how far we've come."

"Mission accomplished."

Mike laughs. Then he sits up straight in his seat, and his voice grows serious.

"Do you remember your first week in the training house?" Mike asks.

My thoughts drift back to that time. The memories are painful, clouded in darkness.

"I don't think much about it," I say.

"I don't believe you," Mike says.

I WAS LOCKED IN A SMALL ROOM.

That's where they put me when I arrived at the training house, drugged and confused. I was overcome with anger and grief, a twelve-year-old boy who had been kidnapped after seeing his father tied to a chair and covered in blood. I was locked up for days while Mother and Father attempted to indoctrinate me into The Program.

But their approach wasn't working.

I shut down. I wouldn't speak or eat.

I knew only one thing.

Mike.

He was the one who hurt my father. He was the reason I was a prisoner.

And I hated him.

One day the door to the room opened, and Mike stepped inside.

"You busy?" he said as if he were interrupting me playing video games.

I looked up at him, seized by two thoughts at the same time.

One: My best friend is here.

Two: A monster is here.

"I brought you something," he said.

He was holding an item wrapped in brown paper.

"Turkey on wheat with avocado and tomato," he said. "And an oatmeal raisin cookie. Your favorite."

"You remember."

"I'm the same guy I was last week."

"Last week you hadn't killed my parents."

He looked at the ground. Was he ashamed? Confused?

Knowing what I know now, it was neither. He was acting.

"You have to eat," he said softly.

He stepped farther into the room and closed the door behind him. He placed the food on a table. He knelt in front of me.

"In war there are casualties," he said.

"War?"

"You have no idea what's going on here."

I shook my head.

"We have to talk, Zach. I need to explain some things to you."

That's when he told me about The Program. Not the story Mother had been telling me, the commander explaining the purpose of the army.

Mike told me the soldier's tale. The story of war from his perspective. What it felt like to be a soldier for The Program. The sense of honor and purpose.

He explained the concept of loyalty—not the kind you have for your school or your favorite sports team, but something deeper, a loyalty born out of hardship and forged in blood.

Loyalty. The essence of The Program.

Mike talked for a long time while I listened. At first, I was confused, but as time went on, I began to understand.

Before he was done, I had eaten the sandwich and the cookie.

And everything was different.

Mike wants me to remember the lesson about loyalty, the reason behind The Program's existence.

I glance at him next to me. His breathing is steady.

"I know the day you're referring to."

"We are soldiers," Mike says. "Never forget what that means."

It's late afternoon now and the sun is high as we turn and wind our way down 96A toward Cayuga Heights. I catch sight of a familiar billboard by the side of the road—a picture of a smiling family sitting at a kitchen table eating dinner. Beneath the family it says:

Home is where the ♥ is.

Steam wafts up from the heart. I used to think this billboard had some greater meaning, but it's just a stupid ad for soup.

Mike says, "I'm going to close my eyes and rest a bit, little brother."

Little brother.

I don't know if Mike saw me looking at the billboard or not, but

I wouldn't put it past him. It's a classic salesman's technique. Create the impression of a relationship whether or not it really exists. This is why car dealers call a potential buyer "my friend." If you create a relationship with words, you create a bond with the person in real life.

Mike and I are brothers.

The Program is our family.

I glance over to see Mike reclining his seat, his eyes shut.

Closing your eyes next to an assassin. It's an act of absolute faith. Or stupidity.

Mike is not stupid. He's sending me a message.

You are my brother, and I trust you with my life.

"Let me know when we get close," he says.

I turn up the air-conditioning to cool off the car. A moment later Mike's breathing deepens and he falls asleep.

IT TAKES A LITTLE OVER AN HOUR TO GET TO CAYUGA HEIGHTS.

I roll down my window when I pass the city limits, taking in the sights and sounds of this new place. I am trained to be adaptable, my energy adjusting to locales without any thought on my part. By the time I turn onto Triphammer Road, I am driving like a local.

I follow Triphammer until it turns into Route 34 in the town of Lansing. The houses are more isolated here. When I get to the address Mike gave me, I find a long, narrow driveway that disappears into a bank of trees.

I continue past for a mile and a half until I find a recessed area in the woods where I can wait out of sight from the main road.

I reach over to wake Mike, but his eyes are already open.

I say, "We passed the house a while back. Not much to see from the road."

"Do you want to wait for nightfall or go in now?"

"It's a toss-up."

"Every minute he's in there is a minute they might break him."

It's a good point. On one hand, there is safety in darkness. On the other hand, time is our enemy.

"Let's go in now," I say.

Mike looks pleased with my choice.

"Do you have anything on the house?" I ask. "Maps, diagrams?"

"Nothing," he says. "You have to go in blind."

It's not ideal, but it doesn't trouble me. You might even say it's become my specialty.

A phone buzzes in the car, the double vibration that indicates a secure text message coming in from The Program.

"Is that you or me?" Mike says.

I take out my phone and find a secure text from Mother, indicating she wants a callback.

I lean over and show it to Mike.

"You ran a leapfrog app?" he asks.

I nod, check the stats on my GPS. "The phone has me outside a Chinese restaurant near the Ohio State campus." Four hundred and fifty-seven miles from here.

"That's good. She still thinks you're in Columbus."

"I can put her off for a while, send a text to let her know I'll call her back."

"You're supposed to be waiting for your next assignment," Mike says. "How would you react to her call under normal circumstances?"

"I'd grab it fast because I'd be bored to shit, waiting for her or Father to give me mission orders."

He laughs. "I used to be the same way."

Used to.

I wonder what changed for him.

"I'll call her back," I say. "Do you want to be here?"

"It depends. How good are you?"

Humans behave differently with people around than they do alone. Mike's asking if his being here will change the way I interact with Mother.

"You can stay or go," I say. "It makes no difference to me."

Mike grins. "Initiate the call."

I open the word puzzle app and arrange the letters.

Before I press Play, I frame the phone carefully in front of me. Mother will likely do a video call, and if she sees something that doesn't look like Columbus, Ohio, on-screen, it will give away my location. So I make sure there are no landmarks or signs behind me, and I start the call.

The word puzzle app disappears. A moment later Mother is on the screen, watching me.

"How's my favorite son?" she says.

I note Mike's eyebrows rise slightly beside me.

Favorite son is nonstandard phrasing. Mother is admitting she has other children, comparing us with one another. She does not do this.

Mother watches me carefully on-screen, gauging my reaction.

I smile into the camera. "Your favorite son is great," I say.

I don't know what Mother is up to, but my guess is that it won't take long to find out.

"How's your summer vacation going?" she says.

Vacation. One of the ways we describe the waiting period between assignments.

"To be honest with you, it's a little boring," I say.

"You're anxious to get back to school," Mother says.

"You know me, I prefer to be busy."

Mother brushes the bangs from her forehead. I notice she's wearing glasses with designer frames. I've never seen her in glasses before.

"Are those new?" I say.

Mother grins and adjusts the glasses. "Nice of you to notice," she says.

"We may not get to see each other in person very often, but that doesn't mean I'm not paying attention."

"You're always paying attention."

"Like mother, like son," I say.

Mother looks pleased.

She says, "I'm calling to tell you I can't bring you back from vacation just yet. Things have been—busy—at home. You know how it was when you left."

Mother is talking about the terror attack in Boston. Most of the Northeast Corridor is still on edge after the bombing by homegrown teen terrorists.

Mother says, "If you can stand it, we'd like you to stay there, relax, and enjoy yourself for a while."

"I'll do whatever you think is best."

"That's my boy. Your father and I may even have a surprise for you."

I feel my muscles tense.

"A good surprise, I hope."

"Is there any other kind?" Mother says. "Stay put and I promise we'll be in touch soon."

I can tell she's not going to give me any more information right now, so I move back to the standard script.

"Will do, Mom. Love you."

"Love you, too."

The call ends. I put the phone down.

"What do you think?" I say to Mike.

"Strange."

"Exactly."

"Let's put it in context," Mike says. "She knows about Howard, but not what he was doing exactly."

"She knows he hacked into The Program server and she probably suspects it has something to do with me."

"Right, so how would she react to that?"

"She'd take me off the active list until she could find out the truth. But she wouldn't want me to suspect anything."

Mike nods agreement. "It's not safe for her to send you on assignment until Howard cracks."

"If I were her, I'd stall for time. And I'd try to find out if my operative was loyal or not."

"How would you do that?"

"I'd set a trap."

"Break it down for me."

"Guilty people do stupid things," I say. "The pressure of guilt drives people to expose themselves. So if I were Mother, I'd keep things positive, maybe even make overtures of friendship and loyalty. I'd try to increase the person's guilt. That's what Mother was doing on this call. That's why she broke protocol and said I was her favorite son."

Mike smiles. "Very perceptive," he says.

"So I'm correct. Mother is setting a trap."

I watch Mike's expression. It does not vary.

"You think I'm the trap?" Mike says.

"It's possible."

"If this was a trap, it's already been sprung. You admitted to me that you knew the kid. You admitted he was working with you. That's enough information, isn't it? Enough for me to report back to The Program and for Mother to issue a kill order."

"It's enough. I agree."

"But here we are. And you are alive and well."

"Here we are."

"This is not a trap," Mike says. "It's an opportunity to clear your name."

I lean back in my seat. It's my turn to close my eyes.

"This is kind of nice," I say.

Mike doesn't speak. I'm guessing he's perplexed by my statement.

"I mean being on a mission with you, Mike. Reasoning it out together."

"What can I say? We're Program brothers."

I open my eyes and look at Mike. My former best friend and greatest enemy. Perhaps there's another chapter in our future.

Could we be brothers?

Mike says, "Let's talk about how you're going into the house. I assume you have a plan."

"I have two plans. One with you and one without."

"You'll have to do it without me. That's not a problem, is it?"

"Are you kidding? I work best alone."

I take Mike through the plan that's been forming since I arrived in town. He asks what I might do in different scenarios, and he makes a few suggestions that are helpful.

But there's only so much planning we can do. When it comes down to it, I'm breaking into a secure house with a long list of unknowns. Usually on a mission like this, I would leave nothing to chance.

But in this case, I have to make chance my friend.

MIKE OPENS HIS BACKPACK.

He takes out a black automatic pistol.

"I don't use guns," I say. "You know that."

"Things don't always go according to plan. You might need it as backup."

"I thought you were my backup," I say with a smirk.

I open the car door.

I say, "Keep the gun, and I'll see you in half an hour."

I ease out of the car and silently close the door behind me.

I start toward the holding house, keeping myself in the shadow of the forest.

It's my first time alone after spending half the day with Mike. I play back the unlikely events of the last few hours. Mike told me that my father is dead. Can I believe him?

I look at the house, thinking about what I've been asked to do.

I imagine Howard inside, alone and afraid, not knowing what's happening to him. It's my fault that he's in this situation.

I stop this train of thought.

Feelings of guilt don't belong on a mission. They are a distraction, and distracted people make mistakes.

That's what happened in New York after I opened myself to the mayor and got betrayed by Samara.

It happened again when I was exposed to Francisco's madness in New Hampshire.

Feelings have created nothing but chaos for me, so I set them aside and instead do what I've been trained to do. I clear my head and bring myself into the here and now, my senses aligned with the world around me.

I focus back on the house. It is deceptively normal, a quiet home on a large and private lot on an isolated street.

I start toward it, probing for security devices that might protect the location from intrusion. I'm within a hundred yards when I spot the first one, a small metal box at the base of a tree, likely a seismographic device designed to pick up vibrations in the woods. I scan the area and spot a second device.

My plan requires adjustment.

I take out my phone, set up a voice filter, then dial 911 to report a house fire at this location with people trapped inside. That should get the authorities moving.

It takes eight minutes before I hear sirens in the distance coming closer. Soon after, I see flashing lights as two fire vehicles approach the house. The small truck pulls halfway down the driveway while the larger engine parks across the street. Firemen pour out, several of them split off and head toward the front door.

Two athletic men come jogging out of the house fast, serious expressions on their faces as they meet the firemen. A conversation begins out of earshot.

If there are two men outside, there will be at least two inside. Maybe more.

It's time for me to go in.

With alarms being triggered inside the house, one more is unlikely to attract notice, so I walk right past the seismographic devices and into the backyard until I arrive at the side door.

It's locked. But only for a moment.

IT SEEMS LIKE A NORMAL KITCHEN IN A COUNTRY HOUSE.

I walk across a wood floor, past a rack of expensive-looking cookware and through a breakfast nook arranged with a small table and wicker chairs.

Within seconds I know that something is wrong.

A normal house makes noise—floors groan when you put weight on them, windows rattle in their frames, walls shift and creak.

But this house makes no noise. It is dead silent inside, like the house where I first encountered The Program as a boy.

I move quickly through the kitchen, turn the corner, and find a man in the hallway, gun drawn, watching the front door. I come at him from behind. A pincer move on his neck drops him into unconsciousness before he knows what's happening. I take the gun from his hand before it can hit the floor, and I place it in a basket where it will be out of sight.

I move into the hallway. It's empty, doors set at strange intervals on both sides. I try the first and find the knob does not give at all. It's not a real doorknob, more like the handle on the outside of a locked prison cell.

I try a second door and find the same thing.

I double back to the fallen man and search his pockets until I come up with a set of keys. I retrace my path down the hall, quickening my pace.

I pause at each door, listening, but they are thick and prevent any sound from escaping. I examine the door handles for traces of skin oil. If there is a prisoner here, his cell will have been opened multiple times in the last few days. Sure enough, one doorknob is marked up more than the others. I slip the key into the lock and feel it turn with a satisfying click.

I steel myself for what will come next.

If I'm lucky, Howard will be asleep, and he will never know what happened to him.

But if he is awake?

No matter.

I will assess, and act. I will not speak or look into his eyes. It will be better for both of us that way.

I disengage the lock, and I open the door.

I see a figure sitting on a cot in front of me.

It's Howard.

"Who are you?" a girl says.

There is someone else in the room.

I spin around and find myself looking at a terrified girl around fifteen years old. Her hair is tangled and her face is dirty. She has a black-and-blue mark around her right eye. She's obviously been here for a while.

Howard stands, his body tense with fear.

I see two cots on opposite sides of the room, two young people in front of them, both disoriented.

Why two?

"What do you want?" Howard says.

I do not meet his eyes. I keep my vision at midlevel, just high enough to be sure he does not present a danger to me.

"Why don't you bastards leave us alone?" Howard says.

He doesn't recognize me.

Howard quickly moves toward the girl. He stands in front of her, blocking my path. He's acting bravely, but I can see that his legs are shaking. Typical Howard, taking a stupid but courageous action.

I do not want to think about this. I do not want to remember Howard or the friendship we shared.

Two people. One is my target, the other a stranger.

I hear the front door opening. Voices outside. The men in front of the house are talking to the firemen, assuring them there is no emergency, and trying to sort out the situation. It's likely that another man is searching the woods, checking for what might have set off the perimeter alarm.

How much time before they realize someone called in a false alarm to the fire department? How much time before they rush back into the house with guns drawn, ready to take on whatever threat has appeared in their midst?

I focus back on the room.

One target has become two. I should take them both out now. Quickly. Without any more thought. It's preferable not to have collateral damage on a mission, but it happens.

This is not collateral damage. It's Howard. He's my friend.

I look up for the first time and meet Howard's eyes. He's looking back at me without recognition.

"Howard," I say. "It's me."

He rubs his eyes, trying to focus. It seems like he's under the influence of some kind of drug, maybe given to him as part of the interrogation.

"What do you want?" he says.

He doesn't know who I am, yet he steps in front of the girl, foolishly risking his life to protect her when he can't even protect himself.

Mike sent me on this mission to kill Howard and secure my place in The Program.

I look at Howard and I know I can't kill him. I could never have killed him.

"I have to get you out of here," I say.

"I don't know you," he says.

"You can't remember right now, but we're friends."

"He was in the black room," the girl says to me.

"The black room?"

"That's where they question us. It takes a while to get normal after."

She seems awake and clear, unlike Howard.

"Who are you?" I ask the girl.

"I'm Tanya."

"Are you a friend of Howard's?"

"Sort of. We're both prisoners."

I look into her eyes. It feels like she's telling the truth. But she is not my mission. I can't help her.

"Let's go, Howard," I say.

I extend my hand, but he doesn't take it.

"What about Tanya?" he says.

"I don't know Tanya. I only know you."

I don't know her, and I don't trust her.

But I won't say that to Howard.

"We can't leave her here," Howard says.

Tanya stands in the corner, her face defiant, like she couldn't care less whether we take her or not. She's trying to act tough, but I can see it's a bluff because her lower lip is quivering.

More noise from the front of the house. Agitated voices of the men standing near the front door, probably waiting until the fire trucks are out of sight.

"We have to go now," I say.

"I'm not leaving without her," Howard says.

I hear the front door close. I'm out of options.

"Both of you," I whisper, "follow me."

Howard gestures to Tanya and they come forward. I take the lead, pushing the two of them out of the room, then guiding them quickly back through the kitchen to the door where I entered.

Without a word, the three of us slip out of the house.

I EDGE FORWARD, MOTIONING HOWARD AND TANYA TO FOLLOW.

Suddenly the door flies open behind us and a Program soldier leaps out, practically running into Tanya. He reacts in a flash, seizing Tanya before I can get to her.

Tanya screams, whirls around, and kicks him hard in the shins, looking like a pissed-off girl at recess. The guy howls and hops on one leg, losing his grip on her. I leap forward before he has time to recover and aim a ferocious open-palmed strike to his throat that crushes his voice box, cutting off his oxygen and disabling him.

This soldier is a witness, so I have to finish the job. As he falls, I plant a vicious kick at chest level, hard enough to crush his sternum and the heart beneath it.

The man gurgles and drops to the ground, dead.

Tanya stares at me, shocked by the violence unleashed an inch from her face. "Is he—?"

"He saw us," I say. "I couldn't leave him alive."

"Who are you?" she says.

"A friend," I say. "I'm here to help Howard."

I glance over at Howard, and he's frozen in place, his finger pointing behind me.

I turn to find another Program soldier emerging from the woods, drawn by Tanya's scream. He stands between us and potential escape, a heavy black pistol aimed at my chest.

I can tell by his stance that he is a professional shooter. He is focused and still, even after having seen his fellow soldier put down a second ago.

I move slowly and the gun moves with me, targeting my center mass. He does not shift the pistol from one person to another like someone untrained and afraid. He knows he cannot shoot all of us at the same time, so he will take us out by level of threat, highest to lowest.

"What do we do?" Tanya whispers.

"I have to pee," Howard says.

"Stay calm," I say. "And no peeing."

I'm searching for options but not finding any. I note the soldier's face, and I can see he's working through his own options. Shoot first or ask questions?

If it were me, I'd shoot.

He hesitates. That's his mistake.

I dive forward and down, hoping he will get distracted and lose his first shot.

A shot rings out, but I feel no pain. I look back to Howard and Tanya and find them unharmed.

I steal a glance at the soldier and see him blink twice, then fall to the ground, dead.

Mike is behind him, gun drawn, body set in a perfect modified Weaver shooting stance.

Mike had killed the soldier before he got a chance to fire his weapon. Now Mike's gun is pointing in my direction.

He looks from me to Howard and Tanya. I feel Tanya stiffen beside me.

"They're innocent," I say.

Mike glances at Tanya and sighs.

"That's the difference between you and me, Zach. I follow orders, not my feelings."

Before I can speak again, another Program asset comes tearing out of the house behind us. Mike fires without hesitation, and the guy goes down in a sprawl.

Mike is killing Program soldiers. What orders is he following?

Sirens in the distance now, returning to the house. I imagine the firemen barely left the scene before they heard the shots and came racing back. It won't be long before the police join them.

"God damn you," Mike says. "I have to clean this up now."

Bullets slam into the tree by Mike's side, and he dives for cover. Another asset has come out of the house behind me, and he's shooting at Mike, assuming he is an attacker and automatically directing his fire at the first man he sees with a weapon.

Mike wings him with a shot, but the man doesn't go down. Then a second man comes out of the house and joins the first.

This is our chance.

"Go!" I shout to Howard and Tanya, pushing them forward.

A fusillade of bullets rips up the ground at Mike's feet. He curses and returns fire.

I use the distraction to lead Howard and Tanya through the

woods, racing back to the Accord. I'll have time later to figure out why Mike didn't shoot us, but now we have to get away.

I put Howard in the back of the Accord with Tanya, then I get in the front and start the engine. When I'm sure there are no police vehicles on the road, I pull out and speed away.

We are safe. At least for the moment.

HOWARD AND TANYA ARE IN THE BACKSEAT.

I glance in the rearview mirror and see their heads pressed close as they whisper, conspiring together.

I back my foot off the gas, making sure to stay within the speed limit.

"What are you guys talking about?" I say.

"What happened outside the house?" Tanya says. "Who was that man?"

"That's a story for another time," I say. "We're safe now. That's the important thing."

"I don't feel safe with you," Tanya says.

They are terrified, and they don't know if they can trust me. I need to project a sense of calm.

"You're safer than you were in that prison cell," I say, keeping my tone modulated.

"He's got a point," Howard says to Tanya. "So what's going to happen next?" he asks me.

It's a good question. And I don't have an answer.

I didn't plan on being out in the world with two kids. Now I have to deal with them, try to guess what Mike's next move will be, find a way to keep The Program off us long enough to—

To what?

To find out the truth about my father. That's primary. Keep us safe until I can find out what Howard knows.

I glance back at Howard, checking his eyes. He's still not focusing, his eyes flitting from side to side. Not so with Tanya. She's watching me, her gaze steady, waiting for me to answer Howard's question.

"I got you out of the house," I say, "but the people who put you in there will want you back. I have to make sure they don't get you."

"Who put us in there?" she says.

Is it possible she doesn't know?

I say, "Why don't we save the discussion until we get some food. You guys must be hungry, right?"

They nod.

I check the road in front and behind us. Traffic in this area is too light.

"I have to get us to a more populated part of the state," I say.

"Why?" Howard says.

"There's safety in numbers."

There's nothing illegal about three teens driving in upstate New York, at least during the day. But once night comes, we will be at risk—from The Program primarily, but also from local cops, who might find it strange to see us driving around in the middle of the night and pull us over.

So I head east, where there will be larger towns and more traffic. I need to get somewhere where I can talk to Howard alone and discover what he knows about my father. And I have to find out how well he knows Tanya.

I think about the kinds of places we can stop without attracting too much attention.

Gas stations and convenience stores are likely to have video cameras, even in upstate New York. Hotels are out, too. It's going to be tough for three teenagers to check into a motel without ID.

A diner. That's the best solution.

I drive up 13 toward Interstate 81 and pull off when we get to Cortland, a university town. As soon as I spot a freestanding diner, I drive in and park on the fringes of the lot.

"I'll go in first and check it out," I say. "I'll give you the signal if it's safe."

"And if it's not safe?" Tanya asks.

"That will be pretty obvious," I say.

"Blood spatter on the front windows?"

"Something like that."

"I wish you guys would stop joking," Howard says nervously.

"Sorry," Tanya says, and she puts a hand on his forearm.

I glance at Tanya. She's covering her fear with humor, a sign that she's coming out of shock.

I leave the two of them alone for a minute while I walk through the front door of the diner, scouting the crowd inside. I see students hunkered down over books and some local families having dinner. Nothing out of the ordinary.

"Anywhere you like," a friendly waitress says. "Grab yourself a menu."

I smile to set her at ease. "Thanks. Coffee and water, please. Times three."

I catch Howard's eye through the window and wave him in. I pick a booth on the side where I can view the entire restaurant from my seat, and I wait for Howard and Tanya to slide in across from me.

I look at them up close for the first time. They are dirty and bruised, but I don't see more serious signs of torture. However, coercion takes many forms, psychological and physical. I sense that they are traumatized, so I have to go easy if I'm going to get any information from them.

The waitress appears at the table. She's about fifty, stressed at the dinner hour but with a genuine smile on her face. "How are you kids doing tonight?" she says, dropping off steaming mugs of coffee and glasses of water.

"We're great," I say. "And starving."

"Starving is good," she says. "We specialize in starving. And waffles."

I smile, matching her energy. She glances at Howard and Tanya. Her gaze travels to Tanya's black eye.

"What happened to you?" she says, a hint of concern in her voice.

"We just came from an Ultimate tournament," I say.

"That's the Frisbee game?"

"Yup."

"How'd you do?" she says.

"We got our asses kicked."

"I can see that," she says. "Bathroom in the back if you need it. It's not pretty, but it's clean. And I'll bring you some ice for the eye."

"I'd appreciate that," Tanya says. "And about a hundred Advil."

The waitress laughs. "I think I'm going to like this girl."

"We already like her," I say. That earns me a smile from Tanya.

I want to win her trust because I'm going to have to question her soon. It will make things easier.

"I'd like a big burger," Howard says.

He's eyeing the menu like he hasn't seen food in a long time.

"You want the deluxe with fries?"

"Definitely," Howard says.

"Make it two," I say.

The waitress looks to Tanya. "How about my friend over here?"

"You said the waffles are good?" Tanya says.

"The best."

"Could I get, like, three thousand of them?"

"I'm not sure we have enough butter."

"Then I'll take a double order. And some scrambled eggs. And syrup. And do you have whipped cream?"

"Wow, you sure are hungry, hon."

"I've been running in the heat all day," Tanya says. "I need sustenance."

"Coming right up," the waitress says.

She gives Tanya a wink and heads back behind the counter to put in our order.

I look at Tanya.

"What's the problem?" she asks.

"Try to act natural," I say.

"This is natural. They were feeding us like one protein bar a day in that place. I'm friggin' starving."

"Me, too," Howard says.

The phone buzzes in my pocket. I check the screen.

It's Mike.

I decide not to risk talking to him, at least not until I've spoken to Howard and Tanya and sorted through their stories.

Howard and Tanya are watching me, curious.

"I need to talk to Howard for a couple of minutes," I say. "Would you excuse us?"

"Will you be okay alone?" Howard says to Tanya.

"I guess," she says.

"I'm not worried about her," I say. "Did you see the way she kicked that guy?"

"I was aiming for his balls, but I missed," she says. "My soccer coach would have torn into me for blowing the kick."

I note Tanya's reactions and the things she talks about. I find my doubts about her receding.

I motion to Howard, and he gets up and follows me toward the back of the diner. I take him into the restroom and check the stalls.

They're empty.

I slip a broomstick through the door handle to prevent anyone from coming in without my knowing.

"I don't understand what's happening," Howard says. "Who are you?"

"Let's start at the beginning," I say. "How are you feeling right now?"

"So-so."

"Can you tell me who the girl is?" I say, pointing back toward our booth.

"She's Tanya," he says.

"What's your relationship with her?"

He looks confused as he searches for the right answer. "They put her in the room with me a couple of days ago. They've been interrogating the both of us since then. We kept each other sane. Mostly."

I think about that—the idea that two prisoners would be in the same house at the same time, waiting to be transported. It's plausible.

"They hurt her," he says. "I didn't see it, only the aftermath."

I think about the bruise on Tanya's eye. His story makes sense.

"Howard, do you remember who I am?" I say.

He bites at his lower lip. "You said we're friends, right?"

"That's right."

"I should know," he says, frustrated. "It's right there, but I can't get to it."

"Don't try too hard. It will come back on its own."

Howard stumbles on his feet, then catches himself.

"I think I'm tired," he says.

I open a stall door and sit him down. I gently roll up his sleeve and find the telltale mark of a series of injections at the vein in the crook of his elbow.

"Have they been drugging you?"

"Maybe," he says.

His breathing grows rapid and shallow. He leans over and groans. "What's happening to me?"

"You're okay, buddy," I say, patting his back.

When I first met Howard, I was on assignment at a private school in New York City. He was an obstacle to my mission that I thought I was going to have to get rid of. I had no idea he would become my first and only friend.

Howard wipes snot with his forearm, fighting tears.

I go to the sink and run the tap, wetting a bunch of paper towels.

"Put these on your forehead," I say. "It will help you feel better."

Cool water on the skin. The shift in sensory information helps to bring a person back to the present moment.

He puts the towels on his face, and I see his eyes slowly coming into focus.

"That's good," I say. "Keep breathing."

He takes a deep breath.

"Can you tell me how you got to the house?" I ask.

He shakes his head. I decide to try to jog his memory.

"A couple of days ago you were in a hotel room in New Hampshire.

We were talking on the phone when some people came into your room. Do you remember that?"

"I don't like hotels much," he says. "Slow Wi-Fi."

I smile. That's more like the Howard I remember.

"You found out something about my father," I say. "You were going to tell me."

"Your father—is he dead?"

Mike said my father is gone. If Howard confirms it—

"Dead. That's what they told me," I say. "But you were trying to get to the truth."

Howard struggles to retrieve the memory. "I was talking to you about it on the phone—" he says.

"That's right. What were you going to tell me?"

His face turns red with frustration. "Damn it!"

He punches his thigh.

I close my eyes for a moment and relax. Getting upset with him right now will be counterproductive.

"There's plenty of time," I say. But how much time do we have before Mike—or The Program—comes after us?

I reach to take the paper towels from him, and Howard surprises me by grabbing me around the waist and hugging me tight.

Whatever brave front he's been keeping up in front of Tanya comes crashing down in a flood of tears.

"I'm sorry I can't remember anything," he says. "I want to remember."

"I believe you," I say.

He glances up at me.

"You do?"

"Absolutely."

I look at Howard. He's the same guy I remember from New York and New Hampshire, the one who risked his life to save mine.

"Thanks for getting me out of that house," he says with a weak smile.

He's still got his hands clamped around my midsection.

"Maybe you should let go now?" I say.

He sniffles and wipes the tears from his eyes.

"That's probably a good idea," he says. "It was getting awkward, even for me."

BACK AT THE TABLE, TANYA IS NOSE-DEEP IN A PLATE OF WAFFLES.

"Sorry, I couldn't wait," she says with her mouth full.

She's quite a sight, shoveling in waffles with one hand while holding a bag of frozen peas on her eye with another.

Howard and I sit down and dig into our food.

"Where are you from, Tanya?" I ask.

"Philadelphia," she says between bites.

I do the math in my head. Philadelphia is a four- or five-hour drive from the house where I found her.

"Can you tell me how you got to the house?"

"I was in a park and I felt a sharp pain on my neck, like I got stung by a bee, but then everything went dark. I woke up in the back of a truck, not knowing where I was. I screamed until I was hoarse, but nobody answered me. Eventually I passed out, and I didn't wake up until the doors opened."

"And then?"

"The men pulled me out of the truck, took me into the house, and started to ask me questions."

She lowers the bag of peas. The swelling is down around her eye, but the bruise is an ugly purple-red color.

"Questions about what?" I say.

"About the neighbor."

"Your neighbor?"

"My friend's neighbor. He died last week."

"Why do you think they were asking you questions about him?"

Her voice drops to a whisper. "Because I saw him die."

Howard looks surprised. I can tell he hasn't heard this before.

"We have to get out of here," Tanya says, her eyes suddenly flitting back and forth, fear breaking through her composure. "We have to get away and call the police. They're going to come back for us!"

She tenses in the booth, ready to bolt. I grab her across the table.

"Tanya, keep your voice down," I whisper. "I know you're scared, but you have to trust me."

She looks at me with tears in her eyes.

"Can I trust you?" she says.

"Yes," I say, knowing it's a lie.

Her breathing slows as she settles.

"I have to go to the bathroom," she says.

I glance at her face, trying to determine whether she might run, call the cops, or take any action that could harm us. I'm betting on the bond she and Howard have established in captivity. They're both still traumatized, and she won't want to leave him alone.

"Go ahead," I say. "We'll pay and meet you outside."

Howard gets up, and Tanya slides out of the booth and hurries to the restroom.

"You didn't know about her neighbor?" I ask Howard.

He sits back down. "She didn't tell me."

Before I can ask another question, the waitress appears at the table.

"Which one of you is Zach?" she says.

Howard looks at me, puzzled.

"I'm Zach," I say with a smile, as I slip a steak knife from the table, palming it in my lap, ready to defend us if need be. "How do you know my name?"

I scan the space for danger, my senses firing on all channels.

"Your brother described you," the waitress says.

"My brother?"

She holds out an old cordless phone. "He said it was an emergency and he couldn't get through on your cell."

I take the phone from her hand.

"Sorry about this," I say. "We're having some trouble at home."

She waves me off. "My manager is out, so it's fine." She walks away.

I motion for Howard to be quiet, then I bring the phone to my ear.

"I trusted you," Mike says.

The anger in his voice surprises me.

"Do you know how many men I had to kill?" he asks.

"I'm guessing the answer is 'too many' or 'not enough.'"

"All of them," Mike says. "Our own assets are dead because of you. Then I blew up the goddamn house."

"Why did you do that?"

"To cover the evidence and save your ass."

"Are you sure it was my ass you were saving?"

"What do you mean?"

I glance toward the restroom, checking for Tanya. She hasn't come out yet. I need to stall for time.

I say, "Maybe you destroyed the evidence at the holding house because it implicates you. How did I find out about the house? Who sent me there in the first place?"

"You're going to tell Mother I sent you on a mission?"

"If I have to."

"Do it if you want to give yourself away," Mike says. "Right now, The Program doesn't fully comprehend the situation. They're rushing more assets into the area, but they don't know what they're looking for. Or who."

"Do they suspect me?"

"Suspect? Of course. But they don't know. They asked me to go and check on you in Columbus. Make sure everything was on the up and up."

"What did you tell them?"

"I said I'd be there by morning. You know what that means?"

"Jeni's ice cream at North Market. You're buying."

"Funny guy. It means I have until morning to find you. And finish this. You want to bring yourself down, that's one thing. But you are not bringing me down. No way in hell."

Right now I'm running a checklist in my mind. How did Mike know to call me here? He must be tracking us somehow.

Mother still thinks I'm in Columbus, Ohio. The leapfrog app on my phone is broadcasting locations several hundred miles from here. And we weren't followed when we left the holding house.

That means there's something I'm missing. I decide to try the direct approach.

"How did you know I was here?" I ask Mike.

"If I tell you, that kind of kills the magic."

"So you know where I am, but The Program doesn't."

"Not unless I want them to."

Mike is arrogant. It's one of the few flaws I might be able to use against him.

Tanya steps out of the restroom, her face freshly washed and shining, her bangs hanging low to try to hide her bruise.

She sees me on the phone and hesitates. I signal for her to meet us at the front door.

"You're with them now," Mike says.

"How do you know?"

"Because I know you," Mike says.

"Obviously not as well as you think you do."

I check outside the diner window again.

"I'm coming for you," Mike says. Then he laughs, a hollow sound that sends a chill through me.

If he's coming for us, that means he isn't here yet.

I put the phone down.

"The waitress said the call was for Zach," Howard says. "Is that your name?"

I nod.

"Do I know you?"

"Not by that name. Howard, we can talk about this later. Right now we have to go."

I use a napkin to wipe down the utensils and glasses on the table, removing fingerprints and trace evidence. When I'm done, I do the same with the phone, wiping it from top to bottom, before leaving it for the waitress on top of a pile of money for the bill, along with a sizable tip. If she's questioned later, the goodwill from the tip could mean the difference between her cooperating with authorities and playing dumb.

"The person on the phone wasn't your brother, was it?" Howard says.

"No."

"Was it that guy outside the house?"

"His name is Mike," I say. "He's a dangerous individual."

"I got the idea when he shot those three men."

As I stand up, I wrap the blade of the steak knife in a napkin and slip it into my pocket.

I don't like knives, in general. But I'll use one to save a life if I have to.

Or to take one.

Howard follows me to the front door, where we intercept Tanya.

"Who was on the phone?" Tanya asks Howard.

"A bad guy," Howard says.

I wave thanks to the waitress, indicating the money is on the table. She gives me a thumbs-up.

"Follow me," I tell Howard and Tanya. "Stay close."

I GET US AWAY FROM THE DINER, AWAY FROM WHERE WE HAVE LAST BEEN SEEN.

I drive fast, but there's no way to outrun electronic tracking, and the more I think about it, the more I'm convinced that's how Mike found us. I scan the horizon, looking for a place to pull over. Upstate New York is filled with deep gorges and elevated crests, geographic features that are remnants from the last ice age. When I find the right place, I pull off the road fast, driving up a steep hill, then down the other side, stopping at the base of the valley where a combination of thick trees and hillside might interfere with a satellite's ability to pick up a tracking signal.

I screech to a halt and ask Howard and Tanya to get out of the car.

I start with the interior on the passenger side. Mike could have easily slipped a GPS device into a door handle, in between the seat, under the mats.

Tanya watches me.

"Now's not a great time to clean the car," she says.

"He's not cleaning," Howard says. "You're looking for a tracking device, aren't you?"

"You got it."

"I can help," he says.

"How can you help?" Tanya says.

"I'm kind of a tech whiz," he says.

"*Kind of* is an understatement," I say.

Howard and I pull the car apart, starting with the interior, then moving to the engine block, the wheel wells, any place where a device could be hidden.

We don't come up with anything.

I stop and rethink my approach. If Mike didn't plant a device, then who did?

That's when I remember something Mike said. I asked him if The Program knew where we were.

Not unless I want them to, he said.

At the time, I thought he meant he was tracking us, and he could give them the information. But there's another possibility, a more ingenious one.

The Program could be tracking us, and Mike could be intercepting their data stream.

"I have to search both of you," I say. "Howard first."

He looks at me like I'm crazy.

"Were you dressed the whole time at the house?" I ask.

"They took my clothes at first. Then they gave them back to me."

"That's what I thought," I say.

I motion for him to hold his hands above his head. I pat him down from neck to feet, checking the seams of his clothes, his belt, every possible place The Program might have planted a device. But I don't find anything.

I step back and look at him.

"His sneakers," Tanya says.

"Good idea," I say.

Howard takes off his sneakers and hands them to me. I pull out the insoles and check beneath them, finding nothing. I examine the sneakers, and I notice an imperfection in the Adidas label at the back of the heel.

I pull the steak knife from my pocket.

"What the hell—" Howard says.

I use the point of the knife to dig behind the Adidas label. It looks as if it's been slit open and reglued. I search inside and come up with a small metallic disc.

Howard whistles.

"What is it?" Tanya says.

Howard holds out a hand and I drop the device into his palm.

He says, "It's a miniaturized GPS beacon."

"That's how they found us," Tanya says. "So we can go now, right?"

She opens the car door and gets in.

"Hang on," I say. I grab the door before she can close it. "It's your turn."

"Why me?"

"You were at the house, too."

She sighs and gets out of the car.

"You want me to take my clothes off?" she says.

Howard's eyes widen.

"How about we start with your shoes?" I say. She removes her shoes and passes them to me. I check them over, but I don't find anything.

"Maybe I don't have a beacon?" she says.

"Maybe not. But I'll have to search you to be sure."

"That's fine," she says. "But I have to warn you I'm a little ticklish."

"I promise I'll be gentle."

"Who said anything about being gentle?"

I feel heat bloom in my cheeks. It's rare for me to lose my cool around women, but Tanya seems to have that effect on me.

I start at her head, running my fingers through her soft blond hair. My hand snags on a hair clip.

"I'll get it," she says.

She takes out the clip and hands it to me, hair spilling down around her shoulders.

"I need a haircut," she says self-consciously. "The salon in the prison really sucked."

"Your hair is fine," I say. "I'm going to check your clothes now."

"What are you guys talking about?" Howard asks.

"Your friend's about to feel me up," Tanya says.

"Believe me, my intentions are purely professional," I say.

Tanya grins and raises her arms above her head.

I glance back at Howard. He's standing by the car, watching us. I make a signal for him to turn around.

"No fair," he says.

"Howard—"

"Fine," he says, and he turns his back.

I begin, feeling the collar of her shirt, then her shoulders, moving over her arms, pausing to check the friendship bracelet on her wrist before patting under her arms and down her ribs. She shivers.

"Are you okay?" I ask.

"Why wouldn't I be?"

"Because you're ticklish, remember?"

"I don't feel ticklish right now."

I run my hands across her belly and I sense her muscles twitch under my fingers.

I reach behind, checking the pockets of her black jeans and tracing the seams across her butt and hips, then down her pant legs.

"Did you find anything?" she says.

"Nothing," I say.

I stand up. Our faces are close now.

"You didn't check everywhere," she says.

"I was being polite," I say.

"It's just professional, right? That's what you said."

"Of course."

"Then don't be polite. Do whatever you have to do."

I follow the outline of her chest, moving my hands to the sides and underneath, checking the fabric of her bra. Her breasts are soft and heavy, the breasts of a woman, not a girl.

"You killed that man outside the house, didn't you?" she says. I run my hands up her shoulders and across her bra straps. "He was already knocked out, but then you went further and killed him."

"He saw us. If he survived, he'd be able to identify us. And they'd know who to look for."

"Because they know you?"

"Yes."

"So it was him or us," she says.

"That's right. And I chose us."

She nods like she understands.

My fingers brush against something in the lining of her bra.

"I need you to take your bra off," I say.

"Personal request?"

I smile. "Still professional."

She hesitates. "I like to know a guy's name before I take my shirt off. Call me old-fashioned."

"My name's Zach."

"Do you mind turning around, Zach?"

"Not a problem," I say, and I give her some privacy.

I hear the rustle of clothes. A moment later she places a bra on my shoulder.

"For you," she says.

It's a blue-and-white-striped sports bra. Still warm.

I pat it down, moving to the side where I thought I felt something. I take the knife and cut into the seam of the bra. There, buried in the elastic, is a round disc like the one I found in Howard's shoe. I turn and show it to her.

"They were tracking me, too," she says.

"Are you guys done?" Howard says. "It's been like six hours already."

"We're done," Tanya says.

He turns and looks at the bra in my hands.

"Wow," he says. "I missed the good part."

I hold out the small disc in the palm of my hand. Howard adds the first one to it.

"Two tracking devices. The Program has been following you, and Mike has been following them, intercepting the signal. Maybe redirecting to keep them off our tail."

"The Program?" Tanya says.

"That's the name of the organization that took you. Mike works for them."

"And you work with Mike."

"In a manner of speaking. We were like brothers in The Program."

"Were?"

I think of Mike on the phone earlier.

I'm coming for you.

"Things have changed," I say.

Tanya reaches out and takes the small discs from my hand. She says, "If Mike still works for the organization, why would he be keeping them off your tail?"

"I don't know," I say.

She looks at the beacons up close. "We should destroy these."

"No way," Howard says. "We should plant them somewhere else."

Howard has good instincts now, developed over the last two missions we spent together.

I fold the beacons into a paper towel, and on the way back to the main road, we pass a bunch of construction vehicles parked at a house where work is being done. I slow down and toss them into the back of one of the trucks before driving away.

"That should make things interesting," I say.

"What now?" Tanya says.

"Now we get as far away from here as possible."

I KEEP US NINE MILES OVER THE SPEED LIMIT.

Slow enough to avoid flagging the attention of law enforcement, fast enough to get us away from the diner, from the GPS beacons, and from the holding house. I aim south toward Binghamton, New York. More people, greater safety.

"How did your father die?" Howard says from the backseat.

"That's a little rude, isn't it?" Tanya says.

"It might make it easier to remember," Howard says.

"It was Mike," I say.

"I knew I hated that guy," Tanya says.

"But I can't be sure he's dead," I say. "That's why I asked you about it in the diner."

"Why aren't you sure?" Howard says.

"I thought I saw something when I was young, but sometimes when you're very young and you experience violence, your brain shuts down. You think you remember something, but maybe you remember it wrong."

"Like a false memory?" Howard says.

"Something like that."

I glance at Tanya, who is scrutinizing me from the backseat.

"What's on your mind?" I ask her.

"This isn't about Howard at all. It's about your father."

"Howard was helping me try to find him. That's why Howard was kidnapped, and why I came back for him."

"I thought you came to save him," Tanya says.

She's perceptive. I have to choose my words carefully.

"Howard is innocent," I say. "I got him into this, so I'm getting him out of it."

"So you're saving him," Tanya says, "but finding your father in the process."

"I hope so. Yes."

I glance back and find her crying.

"What's going on?" Howard says. He's as confused as I am.

"What about me?" Tanya asks. "Where do I fit into this plan?"

"You weren't part of the plan," I tell her.

"I want to go home," she says through sniffles. "Right now."

This is a difficult situation. If I let Tanya leave, she'll almost certainly call the police and bring the wrong kind of attention down on us. That's assuming she isn't recaptured by The Program first. Either way, it's safer to keep her with us, at least for the time being. I need to find a way to calm her down.

"I'll get you home as soon as it's safe, Tanya. I promise."

Her crying gets louder. Howard strokes her shoulder to try to relax her, but it doesn't seem to work.

I spot an exit two miles ahead. I can see the ramp in the distance, arching off the main highway and disappearing behind a hill where I can just make out the sign for a small, local gas station.

"I have an idea," I say. "How about we stop for a minute and you call home? You can let them know you're okay and you'll be back soon."

That seems to do the trick. She wipes tears from her eyes.

"Thanks, Zach," she says. "That means a lot to me."

TANYA'S EYES ARE PUFFY FROM CRYING.

I watch her in the waning light of the service station parking lot. She's trying to keep it together.

"My nana must be worried," she says.

"Who's that?" I say.

"I live with my grandmother. I was supposed to spend this week at my best friend's summer house; that's where I saw the thing happen with the neighbor. But my nana is expecting me to call in from time to time."

It's a calculated risk for me to let her call home, but it's a risk I'm willing to take.

While Howard pumps gas, I lead her away, pulling out my phone and prepping it for the call. I can't use a Program app, so I instead open a secure browser. I search online for one of many CID-spoofing sites that allow you to make a call over the Internet with a fake caller ID appearing on the receiving phone.

Once the spoof has been set up, I pass the phone to Tanya.

"Just type your nana's phone number into the box there, and the site will initiate the call."

Tanya hesitates. "What do I tell her?"

"How long since you were taken?"

"Maybe five or six days. I'm not sure exactly."

"And you were supposed to be at your friend's for a week?"

She nods.

I calculate how much time I'm going to need to get us clear of The Program.

"Tell her you'll be home the day after tomorrow."

"Really?" she says. Her face lights up.

The truth is, I don't know what's going to happen, but hope is a powerful motivator. So I give Tanya hope now.

She types in her grandmother's number and the online service does the rest.

"Nana?" she says. "It's me. I'm using my friend's phone."

I hear an old woman's voice responding on the line.

"I'm fine," Tanya says, and then she sniffles, and tears start to stream down her cheeks. "Really, I am," she says. She wipes at her nose. "I've got a little bit of a cold. Sorry I didn't call you sooner. We've been going to the lake every day, and I've been so busy."

She walks away with the phone, and I let her go. I don't need to screen the rest of the call.

I go back to where Howard is gassing up the Accord.

"When did your father supposedly die?" he asks.

"Are you still thinking about that?"

"You said it's what we were working on before I lost my memory."

"That's right."

"I know Tanya had some issues or whatever—but it's okay with me if we keep working on it."

"You're a good guy, Howard."

"You think so?" he says with a shy smile.

"To answer your question, I haven't seen my father in almost five years."

Howard nods, considering it. The gas pump clicks off. Howard pulls the nozzle and screws on the cap.

"So if he died, it was a while ago," Howard says. "And there would be a record of it somewhere."

"Not necessarily."

"People don't just disappear when they die."

"In my world they do."

A station attendant is sweeping trash in the corner of the lot. I motion for Howard to get into the car. I don't want to risk being overheard in public.

Howard settles into the passenger seat next to me, and we close the doors.

"This morning Mike told me my father was dead, and I should stop searching for him. But before you were kidnapped, you found e-mail exchanges between The Program and my father, e-mails that were sent after his supposed death."

"Is it possible the e-mails were planted to make it seem like your father was still alive?"

"It's possible, yes."

"Would Mike know the truth?" Howard asks.

I think about the moment in my family's living room all those years ago, Mike leading me to where my father was taped to a chair and bleeding.

"Definitely," I say.

"You said people disappear in your world," Howard says.

"That's right."

"But their friends and coworkers don't disappear. Your father knew people in the community. There would be questions and concerns."

"It wasn't only my father who I never saw again," I say.

"Your mother, too?"

I nod.

"I'm sorry," he says softly.

"Let's stay focused," I say, urging him on.

"Okay," he says. "If The Program killed your parents, they'd have to plant a story of some kind, something to keep people from investigating."

"A cover story," I say.

"Exactly."

Howard has a good point. My parents were well known in the academic community. They couldn't disappear without a lot of people asking questions.

"I've never looked for a cover story," I say.

"Why not?"

"I'm trained never to question my superiors. They told me what happened, and there was no reason for me to investigate further. In fact, I was forbidden to do so."

"But it's not forbidden for me. I could look it up online, couldn't I?" Howard says.

It's so simple. I can't help but laugh. "I suppose you could."

Tanya climbs into the backseat and returns my phone.

"Is everything okay with your grandmother?" I ask.

"She assumed I was with my friend, so she wasn't worried. And The Program made me call my friend to tell her I was back with my grandmother. So nobody knows where I really am. As long as the two of them don't run into each other, we're fine until the day after tomorrow."

"The day after tomorrow?" Howard says.

"Zach promised I'd be home by then," Tanya says.

I nod, troubled by my lie. It's not that I wouldn't like to get her home. But I don't know what's going to happen in forty-eight hours—assuming we survive that long.

"Two days?" Howard says. "Then we'd better get going."

"Get going with what?" Tanya says.

"Finding out how Zach's father died," Howard says. "I need your phone, Zach."

I hesitate before giving it to him, recognizing that I'm again asking him to do what got him into trouble in the first place. But what option do I have?

The moment I freed Howard and Tanya from the house, I made my choice. There's no going back now.

I pass Howard the phone.

Then I start the car and pull away from the station. A sidelong glance shows Howard handling the phone deftly, flipping screens at a breakneck speed.

"You're anonymized in a Tor browser," Howard says.

"That's right. The searches are secure."

"What about the phone itself? It has GPS, just like those beacons."

"I have an app that broadcasts false GPS coordinates."

Howard whistles. "Sexy. No wonder we're friends."

He presses a few more buttons on the phone.

"What's your father's name?" he says.

"Dr. Joseph Abram."

He types in the name, and the evening takes a very different turn.

A CAR ACCIDENT.

Howard finds the story in less than two minutes. It's a small article from five years ago in the *Star-Gazette*, a local paper that covers several towns in the area.

Two Found Dead After Car Plunges into Chemung River

Howard reads the story out loud.

"A couple from Rochester, a professor and his wife, unfamiliar with the area, were speeding across Fitch's Bridge in Elmira last night when they lost control and went over the side of the bridge."

Howard passes me the phone so I can glance at the accompanying photo.

A group of townspeople stands on the bridge, pointing to a break in the railing. A police vehicle is parked behind them. There are children in the crowd along with a cross section of people who came out to see what all the excitement was about.

The article had been there all along, waiting for me to discover it if I had dared to look.

Hide in plain sight. That's a Program technique. It's always the best defense.

Hide in plain sight. My face burns as I think how well the technique worked on me.

A hand touches my shoulder. It's Tanya, reaching over the back of my seat. She leans forward until her mouth is close to my ear.

"Are you okay?" she says gently.

"Don't do that," I say.

"Do what?"

"Talk down to me like that. I'm not a kid."

"I was just trying—"

"Don't try," I say.

"Right," she says, and she lets go and sits back in her seat.

Howard is staring at me.

"You guys don't have to worry about me," I say. "I'm a soldier. I've been through a lot of things."

"But it's your parents," Howard says.

I feel my jaw tighten.

"I'm trained to deal with all scenarios," I say.

Neither of them says anything after that.

We drive for a while in silence.

My mind is sorting through the details of the article. While I know it's only a cover story, it could potentially help me prove or disprove my parents' death. If there was an accident, there had to be bodies. If there are bodies, there will be DNA evidence.

I turn to Howard. "The article mentioned Elmira. That's near Corning, right?"

"We're not too far from there," he says.

"I want to see where the accident happened," I say.

"Sounds like a plan," Howard says.

THE ARTICLE CALLED IT FITCH'S BRIDGE.

According to an online wiki, it's the largest bridge in the area, which isn't saying much. If you were driving this stretch of road at night, you could easily pass over it without knowing you had been on a bridge at all. It's a well-paved, two-lane structure with strong side rails. An accident here would be a tough sell.

I stop our car on the road leading to the bridge.

"Read the end of that article again," I tell Howard.

He scrolls on my phone.

Howard reads: "'Rain earlier this week had swollen the river,' said Sergeant Edward Manning of the state police. 'The current is two or three times normal, so that water was gushing all over. Those poor people didn't have much of a chance.'"

A swollen river, a car that loses control at night.

The perfect elements for a tragedy, stage-managed by The Program.

Tanya says, "Do you really think they died in a car accident?"

"I'm sure they didn't," I say. "But if the accident was staged here, there may be proof of their deaths here as well."

"Proof?" Howard says.

"The bodies," Tanya says.

"Oh," Howard says.

I think about my parents' bodies, buried somewhere in central New York, never visited, never honored. A sensation comes over me, tightening my shoulders and chest, causing my jaw to clench.

Rage.

Against The Program. Against Mike.

"I want to see the accident report," I say.

"Way ahead of you," Howard says, and he passes me the phone.

I'm looking at a PDF of a state police report about the accident. I flip through diagrams of the accident scene, measurements of the skid marks on the bridge, a description of the rusted screws on the side railing that failed from the impact of a two-and-a-half-ton vehicle.

"How did you get this?" I say.

"I infiltrated the state police server. It's got a firewall, but nothing I couldn't defeat."

I scroll to the last page of the PDF. It was signed by Sergeant Edward Manning, the same trooper quoted in the article.

I pass the phone back to Howard.

"This guy Manning. Can you find out where he's assigned now?"

Howard goes to work.

"Troop E, Zone 3," he says. "It's a couple of miles north of here in a place called Horseheads."

"That's ominous," Tanya says.

I start the car and turn us in the direction of Horseheads.

"Are we going there?" Howard asks.

"You bet," I say. "I want to talk to Sergeant Manning and hear what he has to say."

Howard spins the phone on his palm and passes it back to me with a flourish.

"You're crazy good on that thing," Tanya tells him.

"This is just a mobile," Howard says. "You should see me on a laptop."

THE STATE POLICE BARRACKS ARE IN A SMALL, BROWN-BRICK BUILDING OFF WATKINS ROAD.

There is no security and no gate. Not in Horseheads. Not in the middle of nowhere.

There's a simple sign that reads STATE POLICE on the roadside, and the front door is framed by two flagpoles, one an American flag and the other a New York state flag.

Both are flying at half-staff.

"Did someone die?" Howard says.

"Looks that way," I say.

I notice a supply area across the road from the main station. I pull in there and back the Accord into a space.

"Keep it running and keep the headlights off," I say to Tanya and Howard. "We might have to leave quickly."

"There are cops everywhere," Howard says, looking across the road at the barracks.

"Not cops," I say. "Troopers. And it's just their vehicles. Most of the troops are out until the shift changes, and that won't happen for a few hours. So sit tight."

"Got it," Howard says. "I'll keep Tanya safe."

Tanya rolls her eyes.

"Watch the front door across the street. If I'm not back in ten minutes, or if you see anything strange, I want you to get out of here. If you can, drive two miles down the road in that direction and give me ten minutes to catch up to you. But if you think you're being chased, don't stop. Get back to Elmira, pick a diner where there are people, and wait for me there."

"Got it," Tanya says.

"How will you find us if we're in some random diner?" Howard says.

"Once you remember who I really am, Howard, you won't need to ask questions like that anymore."

I get out of the car and head across the street to the police barracks.

The door is locked, but through the window I see a female trooper with thick black hair spilling over the collar of her uniform. She's sitting at a desk, chewing hard on what looks to be a whole pack of gum. I knock at the door and she looks up in midchew, startled.

I smile and give a half wave. She doesn't hesitate to reach under her desk and buzz open the door. The lock clicks and I go inside.

"Is there an emergency?" she says, rising from her desk and meeting me in the middle of the room.

"No emergency," I say. "But I'd like to speak to someone."

"I'm someone."

"It's about Sergeant Manning."

Her face drops.

"Oh no," she says. "Are you David?"

"David?"

"They told me he had a son from a previous marriage. They were estranged."

I don't know exactly what she's talking about, but between the look on her face and the flag at half-staff outside, I'm getting the idea.

"I'm Tom," I say. "I'm a friend of David's."

"Does David know?" she asks. "We've been trying to reach him."

"He's coming from out of town," I say. "But he asked me to stop by since I live in the area. It's an awkward situation with the family. You understand."

"Of course."

"What happened exactly?"

She sighs heavily. "It was one of those freak things. They found him slumped over the wheel of his patrol car. Sometimes even healthy people have heart attacks. That's what the doctor said."

This is why the flags are at half-staff. Sergeant Manning is dead.

"When did it happen exactly?"

"Two days ago," she says. "At least he passed on duty, doing what he loved. If that's any consolation."

I hear a single horn blast outside. A warning from Howard?

The trooper looks up. She heard it, too.

"I'll pass that on to David. And I'll be sure to stop by the house to offer my condolences," I say. I head for the exit.

"What did you say your name was again?" she asks, but I'm already out the door.

I see headlights coming around a bend in the road, approaching fast.

I dart across to the supply area and jump into the driver's seat of the Accord. It's running, just as I instructed.

Howard says, "A truck passed by, then came back a minute later. I beeped to warn you."

"Buckle your seat belts," I say.

The headlights approach the barracks, slowing down as they do. A moment later a black SUV passes by, moving slowly. I wait until it's out of sight, then slip the car into gear and pull out of the lot without turning on my lights, turning in the opposite direction.

I drive away from the barracks. When I think we're clear, I glance in the rearview mirror. Brake lights flash behind us.

We're not clear. We're in trouble.

I jam the gas hard, and all six cylinders of the Accord respond, the sedan accelerating hard.

"Holy crap," Howard says. "What's going on?"

I don't respond, all of my focus on the road as we barrel forward with lights off.

"How can you see?" Tanya says.

I can't see. It's pitch-black outside, streetlights set at long, irregular intervals on this country road. I'm driving blind, using my other senses to navigate. It's a skill I learned as part of my training. Scary enough for the driver, but terrifying for the passengers.

"You can slow down," Howard says. "There's nobody behind us."

"You're wrong about that," I say.

A moment later headlights appear, rapidly getting closer. They light up the inside of our car.

"How did you know someone was back there?" Tanya asks.

I don't answer. I'm doing everything I can to keep us on the road. The speedometer climbs from seventy to eighty. The headlights are still coming up fast.

"They're catching up to us!" Howard says.

I push the Accord harder. Ninety becomes a hundred. At this speed on a country road, the tiniest twitch of the wheel could send us into an uncontrolled spin and flip us.

I think about the irony of dying in a car accident just miles from where my parents supposedly died.

That's not going to happen.

The Accord groans at a hundred and ten. The headlights behind us are close enough that they light up the road in front of me, making it easier to navigate. I sense a sharp curve ahead of us, and I slam the brakes and yank the wheel as we skid around the turn.

I hear the engine revving, the sounds of the tires at the maximum of their functional limits, and the ever-present roar of the SUV behind us.

The SUV's headlights get brighter and brighter, so close they're practically touching our bumper.

And then, suddenly, the lights go out.

It's pitch-black on the road in front of us.

One wrong move and we are dead.

I sense another corner coming up ahead. I'm a few yards in front of the SUV, which gives me the slightest advantage.

I should begin adjusting for the curve, but I don't. I stay at maximum speed, as if I would continue on a straightaway.

I wait for the last possible moment, and then I jerk the wheel and slam the brakes hard, throwing the car into a nearly out-of-control spin.

We lose our grip on the asphalt, the car sliding under me for several seconds before I press down on the accelerator again and pull out of the spin.

Behind us I hear a squeal of brakes, followed by the ugly crunch of metal as the SUV misses the turn, flips, and rolls over several times.

"They wiped out!" Tanya says, excited.

I slow down, the car bleeding off speed until we are below forty-five miles per hour.

I hit a button and my window slides down. Wind buffets the inside of the car.

I listen for engine noise behind us, but I hear nothing.

We are alone on the road.

I turn on the headlights.

"Who the hell was that?" Howard says.

"It was Mike," I say.

"Did you see him?" Tanya says.

"I didn't have to. I know how he drives."

"Not as good as you do," Tanya says.

"I hope he has Triple A," Howard says. "But wait a minute. We got rid of the tracking devices. How did he find us?"

"He knows I'm looking for my father. He must have guessed it would eventually lead me to Sergeant Manning. Hence his untimely death. When we downloaded the police report, it might have triggered something on the computer, so he knew we were heading to the police barracks."

"The report could have had a trip wire," Howard says. "I didn't think of that."

"Do you think Mike's dead?" Tanya says.

At that speed, with that violent of a crash, a normal person would be dead or gravely injured.

Mike is not a normal person.

"I'd guess not," I tell Tanya. "But we'll know soon enough."

I hear Howard yawn in the seat next to me. The adrenaline of the chase is wearing off, and the exhaustion is hitting him hard. Tanya looks even worse.

They're not trained to handle crises as I am. They need sleep and a chance to recuperate.

"Howard, pull up a map on my phone. We need to find a lake."

"Not a great time for a swim," Howard says.

"There won't be any swimming," I say. "Only sleep."

THE WATER IS BORDERED BY THICK PINES ON ALL SIDES.

There's an unmarked forest service access trail barely visible from the main road. I carefully navigate the Accord up the trail and park it out of view of the road.

"It's deserted," Howard says.

"I think that's the idea," Tanya replies.

"But what if there's trouble?" he asks.

"You think we can call the cops for help?" she says.

"We're safe for now," I say, trying to set them at ease. "It's been a long day, and you both need to rest. Howard, it takes time for those drugs to work their way out of your system."

I crack the windows and turn off the Accord. I let the smell of the night air clear my head.

I need to rest, too. It's been a confusing day. Being back in Rochester, meeting Mike again, seeing my father's old research associate...

I reach into my pocket and trace the outline of the security pass I found in the professor's jacket. It's completely unmarked, which means it's unlikely to be a standard University of Rochester pass. I'm guessing it's from another facility where the professor is affiliated.

Something is on the edge of my consciousness, trying to work its way in. Professor Silberstein was my father's closest colleague....

Why would he run when he saw me?

"Where are we going to sleep?" Howard says.

"You're sitting in it," I say.

"When you said we needed to find a lake, I was thinking you meant a lakeside motel."

"That would be nice, but it's too much of a risk," I say.

"So we have to stay in the car?" Tanya says.

"You can sleep outside. But I'm guessing there will be fewer mosquitoes in the car."

"I was hoping to sleep in a real bed," Howard says. "It's been a while."

"Soon," I say.

"Day after tomorrow," Tanya says.

I toss Howard the key fob.

"It's going to get a little chilly. Why don't you pop the trunk and see what you can find."

"Will do," he says, happy to have something to do.

"What about me?" Tanya says.

"Help me collect some branches to put around the car."

"Camouflage," she says.

"You're catching on," I say.

We walk through the woods, scouting foliage large enough to use for cover.

"I've been wanting to talk to you alone," Tanya says. "I'm worried about Howard. He's been through a lot."

"I'm worried about him, too," I say. "And about you, Tanya."

She dismisses the idea with a frown. "I'm tougher than he is."

I'm inclined to believe her.

"I need to know if you're really his friend," she says.

"Why would you doubt it?"

"I know you saved us from that house, and I know you want to find your father. But I don't know anything about you. Not really."

"You already know more than you should," I say. "The fewer details you have, the safer you are."

"You mean in case they catch us."

I don't answer. There's no need.

I find a large branch covered with pine needles, and I begin to trace our path back to the road, erasing tire tracks and footprints as I go.

Tanya follows along with me, picking up branches along the way. She stops suddenly and waits for me to turn around.

She has a large branch in her hand that comes to a point on one end. It's sharp enough to be used as a weapon.

"Look, I'm just going to say it. You're being very nice to Howard because you need information from him now. But if I think you're going to hurt him in the future, I'll do whatever it takes to protect him."

"That's very noble of you," I say. "To put yourself at risk for a stranger like that."

"He's not a stranger."

"Really? You were strangers three days ago."

"Things changed."

"I'm not following."

She clutches more tightly at the branch.

"They wanted to hurt me in that room," she says.

"Hurt you how?"

"Sexually," she says, her voice low. "It's not like Howard could have prevented it. Not if they really wanted to. But he stood up to them and he put himself in danger for me, for a stranger as you say."

It sounds like the Howard I know, foolish and courageous at the same time. It's a terrible combination for a soldier, but it makes Howard a very special person.

"He protected me, and I'll do the same for him," Tanya says. "Do you understand now?"

"I do. And I respect that."

My answer seems to satisfy her.

I gesture at the branch in her hands. "Now, do you mind pointing that spear at someone else?"

She smiles.

"I'm all Robinson Crusoe and stuff, huh?"

"I was thinking more *Lord of the Flies*," I say with a smile.

She laughs and lowers the branch.

We continue backward to the car, erasing our tracks as we go.

When we get to the car, Howard is arranging a pile of items in the backseat. "I found a few things in the trunk," he says.

It's meager pickings. A large blanket, a couple of baseball caps, a few tools.

"The blanket smells like gasoline," he says.

"Better than nothing," Tanya says.

We settle inside the car for the night, the two of them together under the blanket in the backseat. I lower my window farther.

"Can we close that?" Tanya says. "It's getting a little cold."

"Have you smelled Howard? We need all the fresh air we can get in here."

"I don't smell any worse than you guys," Howard says.

"You smell fine," Tanya says. "Anyway, I stopped breathing out of my nose an hour ago."

What I don't say is that I need to be able to hear what's going on outside, the telltale crunch of someone walking through the woods, the shuffle of feet sneaking up on us in the night.

Better for them not to know the possibilities, to sleep and heal, to feel safe for the time being, even if that safety is an illusion.

CHILDREN CRY IN THE FOREST.

I hear their voices in the woods around me, a high-pitched sound that grows louder until the cries become screams.

I open my eyes.

It's nighttime. Crickets sing in the forest outside, their calls piercing the night.

I must have been dreaming. I ease open the car door and slip outside, letting the cool air bring me back to reality.

I head into the woods to relieve myself. I'm about twenty feet from the car when I feel my phone buzzing. This is not a dream.

It's Mike.

"You are a terrible disappointment," Mike says when I answer my phone.

He says it so quietly, it sounds like he's inside my head.

"Is it me you're disappointed in, or your driving?" I say.

"It takes a lot of courage to joke when you're this close to death."

My senses are on full alert, monitoring the forest around me. Is it possible that Mike is out there in the dark, watching me?

"I've been close to death plenty of times," I say. "It doesn't scare me."

The neurosuppressor chip that The Program planted inside me throttles my fear, all but removing it from my emotional makeup. On the rare occasion fear tries to grab hold, the chip prevents it from gaining purchase.

I experienced part of a mission without that chip, and I didn't like what it did to me or my performance. That's why I put it back. The Program doesn't know I tampered with their chip. In fact, I'm not supposed to be aware of its existence in the first place.

"Nothing can scare you," Mike says. "I wish I could say the same for your friends. They were very scared."

"Were?"

"Before I killed them," he says.

Could Mike have killed Howard and Tanya in the time it took me to walk a few feet into the woods?

"I don't think they're dead," I say. "I think you're full of shit."

"Would it make a difference if they were dead? Would it break your stupid allegiance to that kid? Tell me why you're choosing strangers over your family."

"I haven't chosen," I say. "Not yet."

Mike is convinced of my motives, but I want him to question himself.

I can hear him breathing on the line. I imagine he's strategizing now, trying to stay ahead of me. I seize the initiative.

"You could help me, Mike."

"Help you how?"

"Tell me about my father."

"I already told you what you wanted to know."

"You told me that you killed him. Now tell me about the accident on the bridge."

"It was staged after the fact. A convenient excuse."

If that's the case, why was Sergeant Manning killed just days before I got here? There are no coincidences on missions. Not when The Program is involved.

"My parents are dead, but they weren't killed in the accident. That's what you're saying?"

"That's right."

"Where are they buried?" I say.

"Are you going to dig up the bodies? Christ, what's it going to take with you? You need a DNA sample?"

"I need the truth."

"You're a confused individual," Mike says. "I suggest you get rid of your friends' bodies, then decide what you're going to do next. Because you are alone out there, Zach. More alone than you've ever been."

"I'm a hunter," I say. "I'm used to being alone."

I disconnect the call, and I take off running back to the car.

When I get there, I see Howard and Tanya slumped together in the backseat, under the blanket.

I throw open the door, and I place my hand on Howard's chest, afraid I'll find—

He's not dead. He's asleep. I feel the comforting rise and fall of his breathing.

He stirs, and his eyes open.

"Everything okay?" he says, his voice heavy with sleep.

"Now it is. Go back to sleep, buddy."

He closes his eyes and snuggles into Tanya's side, like a child cuddling with his mother. I watch the two of them as they sleep.

Feelings are dangerous. Feelings put me at risk.

I close the door, then get back into the front of the car and settle into the driver's seat.

I look at the dark forest around us. I imagine our location on a map grid.

Mike is somewhere on that grid, tracking us.

Howard whispers from the backseat, breaking my concentration.

"Are you up, Zach?"

"Yeah."

"Thanks for taking care of Tanya and me," he says.

"Get some rest, okay?"

"Okay."

Eventually his breathing deepens and he falls asleep. I listen to him snore for a while and then my eyes grow heavy and I drift off to sleep, too.

I'VE SLEPT TOO LONG.

By the time I awake, the birds are singing and the sun is bright. It feels like eight, and I wanted to be up by dawn. Perhaps I've underestimated the toll this mission has taken on me.

I call it a mission, but what mission is it?

Has Mike gone rogue and planned this entire operation without The Program's knowledge? Or is there something else happening that I don't comprehend yet?

I check the backseat. Tanya and Howard are still asleep, Howard curled into Tanya's chest, her arm around his shoulders.

I step out of the car, leaving them to rest a little longer.

The forest is cool, rays of sunlight peeking through the canopy. I walk toward the lake, leaving the protection of the woods to stand on the open bank. I can see the sun shimmering across an expanse of blue-green water.

I hear a car door open and close behind me. I smell her before she arrives, a sweet, warm scent carried by the wind. She smells good for someone who slept in a car overnight.

"Morning," Tanya says, and she comes down to stand next to me. "It's nice to have a minute to breathe."

The two of us look out over the lake, her smell mingling with the scent of water and pine.

"Thanks for talking to me last night," she says. "That meant a lot."

"Sure," I say.

I glance over to find her looking at me with a strange expression on her face. It takes me a moment to understand what I'm seeing.

She likes me.

At least I think she does. Women are strange. They share personal things with you, and then they feel closer to you, even though you've said almost nothing in return.

A bird takes off from the lake, skimming the water.

"The lake is beautiful," she says. She reaches out and takes my hand.

Our fingers intertwine as if we've done this a hundred times before. Her hand feels good in mine.

The car door slams behind us. I quickly pull my hand away from hers.

Howard shuffles down to the lake, rubbing his eyes. He stops when he sees us, staring for a long moment. Then his look turns into one of recognition.

"Your name was Ben when I first met you," he says.

"Right," I say.

"That was in New York. But you had a different name when we were in New Hampshire. You called yourself Daniel."

"Yes."

"At the diner you said you were Zach. Is that your real name?"

"It is."

Howard smiles.

"I remember you," he says.

A NIGHT'S SLEEP HAS DONE WONDERS FOR HIM.

Howard's eyes are clearer, his demeanor completely different from what it was yesterday at the diner. He kneels by the lake and splashes water on his face.

"I remember calling you from the hotel room in Manchester."

"You told me you discovered some information about my father. The last thing you said was that The Program had contacted him."

"That's right!" he says, his eyes widening. "There was communication between The Program and your father. But it was backward, as if your father had been initiating, and The Program was responding."

I glance at Tanya. She's following the conversation.

Should I send her away?

If I allow her to hear this, I'm putting her in grave danger. On the other hand, she was already a prisoner of The Program. How much more danger can she be in?

I say, "What was my father talking with them about, Howard?"

"I can't tell you."

"Because you don't remember?"

96

"Because I didn't get a chance to sort through the data. There was a string of secure e-mails. I could follow the chain of communication, who initiated and who replied, but the contents were encoded. I downloaded everything to my laptop so I could spend some time decoding them later. Unfortunately, later didn't arrive. The Program did. And you know what happened after that."

"So the data we need is on your computer."

"Right. And *they* have my computer."

"They have it, but they haven't been able to crack your encryption software, so they don't know what you have."

"That's awesome," he says. "I wish I had installed a booby trap so it would blow up in their faces."

"Did they have your computer at the holding house?"

"I don't think so," Howard says. "They never brought it into the room to try to force me to log in. That would have been the smart thing to do. Which means they probably sent it to a lab."

I wonder where computers would be sent and how I might access them. I try to imagine some scenario in which we retrieve Howard's laptop, but I don't know the location of any Program facilities, and it's not like I can ask Mike to bring it to us.

"I think we're out of luck getting the computer back," I say.

Howard sighs. "I'm sorry, Zach. I blew it."

"Not your fault," I say.

"I'm not following this," Tanya interrupts. "Your father worked with the people who kidnapped us?"

"There's reason to believe so," I say, "but I need real evidence. Howard, what did they ask you about at the house?"

"They wanted to know about the chip," he says, and he points at my chest, the location of the neurosuppressor that removes my fear.

I think of Howard on my last mission, walking into the bathroom to find me with a knife in my hands, my body covered with self-inflicted wounds as I searched for a chip I wasn't sure existed.

"Did you tell them you knew about the chip?" I ask him.

"No," he says. "I thought it was better not to discuss you at all."

"Good job. Anything else I need to know?"

Howard struggles with the question but doesn't come up with anything.

"You told me they were asking you about a facility of some kind," Tanya says, trying to help him remember.

"That's right!" Howard says. "They wanted to know about a research facility. I kept telling them I had no idea what they were talking about, but they didn't believe me. They wanted to know if you'd said anything about it."

A research facility.

The secretary at the University of Rochester said the psych department had a special research facility downstate.

"Did they mention Corning by any chance?"

Howard's eyes light up. "Corning. Yes! They asked me if I'd been there."

One weekend after my twelfth birthday, my father drove me to Corning from Rochester. He said he'd be working there in the future, but I couldn't tell my mother that he was showing me the place or we'd both be in trouble.

"Your mother doesn't understand that things are getting better," he said to me.

"Better how?"

"More money, more opportunities to do the things I love."

"Why doesn't she understand?"

"She's afraid," my father said. *"She doesn't want anything to change."*

"I don't want anything to change, either."

"My father took me to Corning once," I say. "A long time ago."

That was a short time before Mike came into my life and things changed forever.

The memory gives me an idea.

"Howard, what would it take to get into the computer again?"

"My computer?"

"No, The Program's computer."

"You mean the server. They have the most complex security protocol I've ever seen. I'd need a week in a secure location with all my equipment. Then maybe I could hack through their firewall."

"What if I could get you access directly into the server?"

"If you can get me in, I can retrace my steps. If I get a little time, I might be able to retrieve the information, and we could sort through it together."

"All right, then," I say. "I have a plan."

I reach into my pocket and pull out the white security badge I took from Silberstein's jacket.

I pass it to Howard. He flips it back and forth in his hand.

"It's a mag-stripe security pass card," he says.

"Can you get the information off it?"

"I need some equipment," he says. "A mag reader of some kind. I might be able to adapt a POS system."

"Too many initials, Howard."

"Point of sale. You know, like a credit card reader or a payment system in a restaurant."

"Let's get going," I say. "I'm sure we can find one on the way to Corning."

WE PASS A CONVENIENCE STORE THAT LOOKS PROMISING.

It's a small store, no cameras or security of any kind. There's a credit card reader next to a register manned by a bored-looking teenage clerk.

I motion to Howard and Tanya, and they follow me through the front door.

I gesture to the credit card reader by the register. The clerk is standing practically on top of it.

"Will something like that work for you?" I ask Howard.

"Maybe. But how can I use it with the guy standing there?"

"I've got this," Tanya says.

She smiles and walks toward the counter. I notice a flirtatious sway in her hips that wasn't there before.

"Holy crap," Howard says. "What happened to Tanya?"

Obviously, he notices, too.

"Can you help me find something?" Tanya says to the clerk. His eyes almost pop out of his head when he sees her.

"S-s-sure," he stammers.

A few seconds later, she has him all the way in the back of the store, combing through a high shelf that looks like it hasn't been touched in half a century.

"Go," I say to Howard, urging him toward the register.

I stand between Tanya and the register, using my body to screen whatever Howard is doing behind me. I hear beeps from the credit card reader, Howard cursing under his breath, and the sound of things being plugged and unplugged followed by more beeping.

In the back of the store, the clerk is taking down a box of cereal for Tanya.

"How much longer?" I say over my shoulder.

"Thirty seconds," Howard says.

"Hurry," I say.

Tanya glances at me and I give her the sign to keep the conversation going.

She acknowledges silently, then thrusts out a hip and starts asking the clerk questions that have him shuffling nervously in front of her.

"Almost there," Howard says. "I just need a pen."

"Is there one on the register?"

"Oh yeah, I found one."

I hear him scribbling on a piece of paper, then he comes bounding out from behind the counter just as Tanya and the clerk come walking back up the aisle.

"Who's this?" the clerk says, surprised to see us there.

"These are my brothers," Tanya says.

"You guys live around here?" he says.

"Upstate," I say. "We're just passing through."

"Too bad," he says. "It's good to meet new folks. It's kind of a small town, you know. It gets boring. My mom would probably invite you over to dinner."

"That would be nice," Tanya says. "If we come back this way, I'll drop by and say hi."

"Great!" he says.

I palm out cash for the food, and we get out of there fast.

"What did you get, Howard?"

"An address," he says.

"I got crunchy granola," Tanya says. "And a guy's phone number."

"We'll get to you in a second," I say.

Howard passes me a sheet of paper with a name and a Corning address on it. Some place called the Mercurio Institute.

"Have you heard of it before?" he asks me.

"Never," I say. "But I have a feeling I'll recognize it when we get close."

"How did you get that info from a credit card reader?" Tanya says.

"Creativity," Howard says with a grin. "How did you get that guy to leave his register unattended?"

"The same," Tanya says.

"If you two are done high-fiving each other, I'd like to get on the road."

I WAS RIGHT.

The closer we get to the Mercurio Institute, the more I remember visiting when I was a boy. I recall science labs filled with signs and symbols my father had to explain to me. It was like a giant playground for me at the time. I doubt it will be like that now.

As I drive, I trust my memory and intuition, letting it guide me through the streets of Corning, through the center of town where I had lunch with my father so long ago, and along Powderhouse Road until a facility comes into view.

I pull off the road and study it from a distance.

There is a high fence around it that did not exist back then, and a military-style guardhouse at the entrance where cars must stop to gain access. The one building I remember has grown into three. I note people moving along paved walkways. A small placard next to a doorway reads MERCURIO INSTITUTE with no other identifying information.

"We're going inside, right?" Tanya asks.

She's kneeling in the backseat, looking over my shoulder at the view out the front window.

"Howard and I are."

"What about me?"

"You'll stay here on watch."

"I don't think so."

"Why not?"

"In the movies, the one on watch always gets in trouble."

"That's true," Howard says. "I've seen those movies, too."

"What are you talking about?" I say.

"You know how it is," Tanya says. "Someone from the group keeps watch while the others break into the place. It seems like the plan is working until the one on watch gets knocked out with a rifle butt."

"That's in the movies, not reality," I say.

"How do you know it's not reality?" she says.

I glance over my shoulder at Tanya. She stares back at me, stubborn, her jaw set tight. For a moment she seems older than her years. Then she makes a silly face and I remember how young she is. Maybe just a couple of years younger than me, but still, she's a kid, and I am—

"So can I come?" she says.

It could be beneficial to have her with us. If we are discovered inside, two boys alone are more threatening than two boys with a girl. And the thought of all three of us together gives me an idea about how we might get in.

"Come on," Tanya says. "You don't want me to get knocked out by a rifle butt, do you? My nana paid a lot of money for Invisalign braces. I don't want these beauties to get messed up."

She smiles wide, revealing perfect teeth.

"Okay," I say. "You can come."

"I told you he'd let me," she says to Howard, like she planned it all along.

THE LAST THING THEY WOULD EXPECT IS FOR US TO DRIVE UP TO THE GATE.

So it's exactly what we do.

"Everyone relax when we get to the guardhouse," I say under my breath.

"Driving toward a man with a gun is not very relaxing," Tanya says.

"No kidding," Howard says. "I feel like I have to pee and throw up at the same time."

Tanya whispers something to him, and I see him relax slightly.

I stop at the guard booth. There's one man inside, his uniform shirt bulging at the arms. He takes one look at us and practically goes cross-eyed.

"Good morning," I say, in a friendly voice.

"You must be lost," he says.

"Nope. My dad works here."

"Your dad?" he says, not believing me.

"Of course. I'm Joshua Silberstein," I say.

First calculation. Silberstein got spooked after seeing me, and he ran to where he'd be the safest. Second calculation. His son is not going to be recognized by the guards because he never comes down here.

"You're Dr. Silberstein's son?" the guard says.

"Baseball player extraordinaire, good with the ladies. I'm sure you've heard about me."

The guard laughs. "We've heard," he says.

He looks into the back of the car.

"And who are they?"

"My friends. Dad said I could bring them for the tour."

"Tour?"

"We're doing a summer school project. Also Dad forgot his security card again. My mom said to take it to him and tell him he'd forget his butt if it wasn't attached. Between you and me, I'm not relaying that part of the message."

The guard takes the card, swipes it on some sort of device, then hands it back to me.

"Your dad is here," he says.

"Would you mind telling him that Joshua is on time, as requested?"

If the guard were smart, he'd ask for ID right now, and when he didn't get any, he would order me to back up two hundred feet from the gate, call out men to search us, and lock the place down until he figured out what the hell was going on.

That's if he were smart. But he's not smart. He's so thrown by the appearance of three teenagers at the gate, he does the opposite of what he should.

He picks up the phone and calls Professor Silberstein.

Third calculation. Silberstein is scared after yesterday, and his son appearing at the gate is going to throw him. He won't follow proper security protocol when he hears Joshua's name.

The guard turns away from me, speaking into the phone for a minute before hanging up. After a moment he turns back around.

He says, "When you get inside, pull up to your left and wait. Don't get out of the car. Your dad is coming out to meet you."

"Fantastic. Thanks," I say with a smile.

And the gate opens in front of us.

THE NEXT MOMENTS WILL BE CRITICAL.

Silberstein will come out of the building, and one of two things is going to happen.

He's going to run. Or he's going to freeze. I'm hoping for the latter.

I'm in a car he won't recognize, and that will confuse him. If I can keep him from seeing me for long enough, I might be able to pull this off.

I wait for the door of the building to open.

It's Silberstein. He's alone.

He begins walking across the parking lot toward us.

I turn around so I'm facing Tanya, showing Silberstein the back of my head.

"Talk to me, Tanya."

"About what?"

"Anything. We just need to be in conversation as he comes toward us. Then do what I tell you, okay?"

"Okay."

I glance at Howard in the back. His eyes are clear and his energy is better. The drugs have worked their way out of his system. That's good, because I'm going to need him in full form once we get inside.

"Look over my shoulder, Tanya. Is he walking toward us?"

"Yes."

I make sure my window is lowered all the way. I relax my posture and let my shoulders move around as if I'm distracted and in conversation.

"Give me a countdown," I say.

"What am I counting?" Tanya says.

"Number of steps until he reaches the car."

"About twenty steps," she says with a whisper.

"How does he look?"

"Confused."

"Perfect."

"Ten steps."

"Whatever happens, I want you guys to stay calm," I say.

Tanya lowers her voice. "He's here in three, two—"

"Joshua?" I hear Silberstein say from outside the car.

I turn quickly, reach out and grab his belt buckle, and yank him hard up against the side of the car.

He gasps, startled, and tries to pull away.

He reaches down to free himself, and I grab him by the wrist and jerk him down until I can get hold of his shirt collar and pull his face close to mine.

"You know who I am," I say.

He looks at me, and his pupils dilate.

"Yes," he says.

I thought so. He wouldn't have reacted the way he did in the lecture hall unless he knew me.

"If you know me, then you know what I can do," I say.

"Yes."

I sense his fear. So it's not just that he remembers me, he knows about The Program, too.

"You owe me," I say.

"What do I owe you?"

"Information."

"You want to know about your father," he says.

"Right."

"Who are these people with you?" he says. He looks at Howard and Tanya, suspicious. Maybe he thinks we're a hit squad come for him. I can use his reaction to my advantage.

"You're going to take us inside the facility," I say.

"I can't do that."

"You have no choice."

"They won't let you in."

"They already have. The guard thinks I'm your son. He believes you're giving me and my friends a tour today."

"That's ridiculous."

"Do you want to tell him or should I?"

"I still can't take you inside," he says.

I pull his head down farther, lean forward, and whisper in his ear.

"You will die now," I say calmly. "Which means you won't be around to see what happens to your family when I get back to Rochester."

He gasps. "Okay," he says. "I'll do what you want."

"Smile and wave first."

I hang on to one wrist while he stands up and uses the other to wave to the guard, signaling that everything is okay.

"Do we understand each other?" I say.

"Absolutely," Silberstein says. "Park up here on the right. I'll take you in."

If I let him go, he could do anything. Shout out, run for safety, trigger an alert—but I'm betting he won't do any of those things.

So I let go of his wrist.

He walks ahead of us, indicating where to park.

"Are you guys ready?" I say.

Howard and Tanya nod.

"Game time. Follow my lead."

"What did you whisper to him?" Tanya asks.

"Let's just say I made a compelling argument why he should help us."

"You told him you'd kick his ass, right?" Howard says.

I wink at Howard and slip on a baseball cap before I step out of the car. It's nothing like a real disguise, but it may obscure my features enough to slow down any facial-recognition software linked to the cameras inside. It won't keep a sophisticated system from recognizing me, but it might send a few false positives and buy us some time.

For a moment I regret bringing Howard and Tanya with me, exposing them to this level of danger after the things they've already been through.

But it's too late for regrets now. It's time for action.

SILBERSTEIN USES A BADGE TO UNLOCK THE SECURITY DOOR.

"I guess you had a backup," I say, showing him the stolen pass that got us through the guard at the front gate.

"How did you—"

"It was in your jacket at the University of Rochester."

He scowls as I hand it back to him.

We enter unchallenged. There are no additional guards inside, no metal detectors, no cordons to pass through. At first, it seems that security might be lax inside the building, but then I notice the coded locks on every door. There is logic behind the design. I imagine warrens of buildings, departments, offices, each secured from the others and limited by different levels of access. Nobody can enter a door unless that person is previously authorized.

It's called atomization, and it's one of the most effective security protocols that exists.

Silberstein leads us down a bare hallway. There are numbers on the doors, but no other signage to speak of.

"You found this place," he says, "so I imagine you know where you are."

I could bluff and pretend to have knowledge I don't have, but that could be counterproductive. If someone suspects you know more than you're telling, they'll be careful about what they say, fearful of telling you too much or leaving out what they think you already know.

So I say, "I came here once with my father when it was being built. Beyond that, I know nothing."

A woman comes down the hall toward us, her expression changing to surprise at discovering the strange group of people in front of her. Silberstein gives her a friendly smile. *Look what I'm stuck doing today.* She stifles a smile and continues by without comment.

"We'll talk when we get inside," Silberstein says under his breath.

We stop in front of a door with a number on it. Silberstein touches his pass to a white square on the wall, then keys in a code; the door clicks. It's a dual security measure. *Something you have + Something you know.* This way if a pass is stolen, it alone does not provide access. Not unless you also have the code.

The door opens to reveal a small computer lab. Silberstein guides us inside, making sure to close and lock the door behind us.

Once the door is closed, Silberstein slumps down in a chair.

"You're Zach, aren't you?" he asks.

I nod.

"I knew it," Dr. Silberstein says. "I haven't seen you in almost five years, but I guessed it was you the moment you walked into my lecture hall. You look just like your father."

"That's why you called for help at the university?"

"What are you talking about? I didn't call anyone."

So Mike was telling the truth. Nobody tipped him off. He antici-pated my visit to the U of R and got there before me.

"Who are these kids?" Silberstein says, looking at Howard and Tanya.

"Friends of mine."

"How long have you known them?"

"Forever," I say.

He looks at them warily.

"Let's put it this way," I say. "I trust them a lot more than I trust you. So why don't you tell me what's going on in this facility."

"You said you had been here once before," he says.

"That's right. It was one building back then. None of this security."

"The building you visited with your father was the beginning of a sea change in our research philosophy."

"Our?"

"Your father's and mine. We were research partners. What began as a simple testing facility grew into the finest psych research center of its kind. This place is your father's legacy."

"If that's the case, where's my father?"

He winces at the question.

"I'm sorry, Zach. For everything."

"What do you have to be sorry about?"

"About your parents—" He hesitates. "The way things happened."

"You mean the way they died?"

I'm hoping he will contradict me, tell me they're not dead, tell me the story I've been led to believe is not true.

But he doesn't do that.

He simply says, "Yes."

"What did you have to do with their deaths, Dr. Silberstein?"

His demeanor changes completely. His breathing grows rapid, and his eyes flit around the room, skimming over Howard and Tanya before returning to me.

"I caused their deaths," he says.

The muscles in my shoulders tighten, rage rising inside me.

"Indirectly," he adds quickly. "Zach, you have to understand, your father was a genius. His discovery was unparalleled."

I look at him, not comprehending. He realizes I know a lot less than he thought I did. I see him sorting through information now, preparing to spin the story.

"Don't do that," I say. "Don't change the story in any way. Tell me everything."

Silberstein continues, "We were studying post-traumatic stress disorder."

"PTSD," Tanya says.

"Exactly," Silberstein says. "During trauma, pathways in the brain become imprinted by traumatic events. That results in a kind of stress reaction in the brain, one that is experienced again and again, replaying long after the events have ended. Your father was searching for a way to break the cycle before the imprinting could take hold."

"How could he do that?"

"By taking away fear."

I hear men's voices in the hall. Silberstein does, too, because he stops talking. After a moment footsteps pass by the door without incident.

I glance across the room. Howard has set himself up in front of a computer monitor and he's typing away.

"Be careful over there," Silberstein says.

"How many false keystrokes before it locks down?" Howard asks.

"Five," Silberstein says, a little surprised. "How did you know that?"

"Even my iPad resets itself after ten bad login attempts."

"Give him access," I say.

"Why?" Silberstein says.

"He's a genius," I say. "Like my father."

I've never thought of that before, but it's true. Howard reminds me of my father, or at least what I imagine my father might have been like when he was a kid.

"I can't let him in," Silberstein says.

"You can and you will," I say.

"There is classified information on our server."

"I'm guessing you have a military contract. That's why there's so much money available for the psychology department."

He nods. "DoD," he says.

The Department of Defense.

"I'll lose my job if I give your friend access," he says. "I could go to prison."

"You're about to lose a lot more than your job," I say, rising from my seat.

Silberstein gets up quickly, leans over the desk in front of Howard, and keys something into the terminal. Then he steps away.

Howard taps at the computer. "I'm in," he says. "I just need a thumb drive."

"No way," Silberstein says.

"Check his desk drawer," Howard says.

Tanya opens the desk, searches around for a moment, then holds up a small stick-like device.

"Perfect," Howard says.

Silberstein paces the room now, growing more agitated by the step.

"You said my parents' deaths were your fault," I say, bringing the conversation back around.

"I didn't say that. I said I had something to do with them. Indirectly."

"What did you have to do with it?"

"You have to understand, we were small-time academics running a PhD program. Totally under the radar."

"But something happened."

"Opportunity," Silberstein says. "At first, it was a single grant. It seemed like the source was benign, an obscure foundation. As time went on, we were offered additional money, more prestige. And then the agenda started to change. The donors began to throw their weight around. They wanted us to apply our research to understanding why young soldiers were returning from war with such terrible psychological trauma. Your father didn't like what was happening. He thought we were losing control of our own research."

"He didn't like it, but you didn't have a problem with it?"

"It was an opportunity to expand the good work we were doing and grow the department at the same time. It seemed like a beneficial trade-off to me. But your father had this stupid obsession with remaining independent. He believed the only real research was pure research, unencumbered by other agendas."

"So he resisted."

Silberstein nods.

"Neither of us realized who we were dealing with. By the time we knew, it was too late."

I look around the lab at the state-of-the-art equipment and high-end furniture.

"It looks like you got what you wanted," I say.

Silberstein's face is tormented. "I never wanted your family to be harmed."

I hear footsteps outside the door again, but this time they don't pass by. There's a loud knock.

I leap up. "What did you do?" I say.

I pull his chair back with him still in it and examine the space where he was sitting. I squat down and look under the desk.

There's an alarm button under the lip of the table. A button he'd obviously pressed.

"Did you get what you needed?" I call to Howard.

"It's a complex system," he says. "I could use another ten minutes."

"I can get you five," I say.

I glance around the room, searching for anything that might be used as a weapon.

Another knock at the door.

"Let them come in," Silberstein says. "They won't hurt you. Not when they find out who you are."

That means they don't know who I am yet. They only know an alarm has been triggered in the lab.

I head for the door.

Silberstein says, "Please, Zach. You don't want to mess with these guys."

"On the contrary," I say. "I really do."

I turn to Tanya. "Stay in the room, lock the door behind me. Don't open it unless you know it's me. I'll knock a pattern, five and three."

"What if someone breaks in?" Howard says.

I look from Tanya to Howard. I don't have a weapon to give them, and I can't expect them to defend themselves.

I say, "If they force their way in, do whatever they tell you to do."

"What if they take us somewhere?" Howard says.

"I found you before, didn't I?"

"We'll be okay," Tanya says, calming him.

I've seen her stay cool in several tough situations. I have no reason to doubt her now.

I set myself in defense mode. Then I open the door and slip outside, not knowing what I will find, but knowing I must be ready for anything.

THREE GUARDS WITH GUNS ON THEIR BELTS.

They are a few feet from the door, huddled together and strategizing.

That gives me the element of surprise.

The first guard is easy, I step in fast and use his body as a weapon against the second guard. The two of them topple to the ground, disoriented.

The third man reacts quickly, jumping away from me and drawing his weapon in a single motion. I do what he will least expect: I move forward, shrinking the distance between us in less than two seconds.

"You guys scared the crap out of me," I say, making my voice high and afraid.

He blinks at me, confused. A minute ago he saw me take down his two fellow security men, and now he sees me acting like a kid. His brain can't process it.

That's exactly what I'm counting on.

"Stop," he says.

But I don't. I walk up to him and take the gun out of his hand.

He is startled, so much so that it takes him a second to realize what happened.

"What the hell?" he says.

By then it's too late. I strike at him, using the weight of the gun in my hand to deliver a forearm shiver to his chest, hard enough to rattle his teeth.

"How many are responding?" I ask.

He doesn't answer, so I hit him again. That gets him talking.

"One team responds to verify and report in. If there's an actual problem, they send more."

"There's no problem," I say.

"But I—"

"Make the call."

I point the gun at him. I have no intention of using it. It's a signifier, the symbol of danger that makes the threat more real. He doesn't know it, but I am a lot more dangerous than this weapon.

"Make the call," I say.

"Forty-three reporting," he says into his radio.

"Forty-three, go," the voice replies.

"Code red area seven—" he shouts.

I bring the butt of the gun across his temple, sending his head careening into the wall and knocking him out cold.

Whatever he communicated has turned the false alarm into an actual alarm.

Nothing I can do about it now. I turn and run back toward the computer lab where I left Howard, Tanya, and Silberstein.

The fight earned Howard an extra five minutes on the computer. I hope it was enough.

I knock, five and three, as I arranged.

"It's me," I say through the door.

There's no response.

I knock again, identify myself again.

I hear Tanya scream inside the room.

I rear back and kick the door hard below the locking mechanism.

Another scream, longer and more terrifying.

Then a gunshot.

I kick again, below and above the mechanism, weakening the structure before flinging myself through the door.

It's not what I was expecting. It's much worse.

THERE IS BLOOD.

A pool of red, slowly spreading across the floor. Silberstein is sprawled on the ground at Tanya's feet, his head at an unnatural angle, the side of his skull blown open from a gunshot wound.

Tanya is holding a black .38-caliber pistol. It's pointed at Howard, who is cowering in a corner across the room.

"Tanya?" I say.

Her expression is calm. The gun is steady in her hand, her grip firm but light. It is the grip of someone experienced with firearms.

"What's happening here?" I ask, keeping my voice low.

First action: Engage her in conversation to stall for time.

Second action: Neutralize the threat.

I note the angle of the weapon. Half a turn in one direction, and Howard is in her sights. Half a turn in the other, and it's me.

I need to distract her, buy myself another moment of assessment time. Move myself into a better position for what I'm about to do.

I slide a step to the right.

"Stop, Zach," she says.

I stop.

"I want you to understand—" she says.

"I do understand," I say.

Her stance, her comfort with the weapon, the blood on the ground at her feet.

Tanya is not who she says she is.

"The professor pulled a gun out of the drawer," Tanya says. "I had to act."

"She grabbed his arm," Howard says. "She kept him from shooting me. She saved my life, Zach."

"We were fighting for the gun and it went off," Tanya says.

I appraise Silberstein's body, its position on the ground, the gunshot that has sheared off the side of the man's head.

I look at Tanya. If a normal girl had just killed someone, she would be shaking and flushed.

Tanya is not flushed.

A normal girl would be in shock, her eyes glazed, her pupils dilated.

Tanya's eyes are calm. And she is still holding the gun in firing position, halfway between myself and Howard.

Tanya is an assassin.

"Your move, Tanya."

She looks from me to Howard, struggling with something internally.

"What's happening?" Howard says. He doesn't understand my reaction. Maybe he thinks Tanya got lucky and shot the professor by accident.

I judge the distance between Tanya and myself. She is close, but not close enough for me to get to her and disarm her before she wreaks havoc. Not if she's as good as I think she is.

"Zach."

She turns toward me, and something shifts in her energy. She relaxes from a state of readiness. She spins the pistol, flicking on the safety before extending her arm and offering me the gun.

A moment ago she killed a man and it looked as if she was going to do the same to Howard. Now she's surrendering the weapon.

It makes no sense.

"Trust me," she says.

"That's a little bit of a stretch given the circumstances," I say.

"Then trust your instincts."

My instincts led me astray. Tanya is dangerous, and I missed it. I had doubts about her at the beginning, but they were put aside by other feelings.

Dangerous feelings.

The gun is in her outstretched hand, butt end facing me.

I take it from her and slip it into my waistband.

"We can't stay here," she says.

She's right. We have to get moving, or we will be trapped.

"Howard, did you get what you needed from the server?"

"Got it," he says, and he pulls a thumb drive from the computer and pockets it.

"Then let's get out of here," I say.

"Silberstein—" Howard says.

"He's gone," I say.

I reach down and grab the security pass from his body.

I head for the door, pulling Howard with me.

"What about Tanya?" he says.

I look back. Tanya is standing in the middle of the room, watching me.

"Can I come with you?" she says.

"Why would I allow that?"

"You can't leave her here," Howard says.

He still doesn't understand who we're dealing with.

I hear footsteps running through the hallway outside. Soldiers are approaching in response to the guard's emergency transmission. Normal protocol would be to lock down the facility, keep the scientists safe in their offices until the guards can search the entire building and secure the premises.

"You need me to get out," Tanya says.

"I don't need anyone," I say.

"It will be easier with me. You know it will."

She's right. The presence of a woman diminishes the perception of threat. In her case, that would be a very wrong perception, but the guards won't know that.

Tanya is dangerous, but she turned over the gun and made herself vulnerable to me. She wants to stay with us now. I just don't know why.

Footsteps approach the door.

"They're coming," Howard says, his voice high-pitched.

I have to make a decision. Take Tanya, or leave her.

"We go together," I say.

"Thank you," Tanya says.

"Don't make me regret it."

She crosses the room to join us.

I listen at the door, creating a mental map of what we will find when we step into the hall.

"How are we going to sneak out of here?" Howard says.

"No sneaking," I say. "We're going to walk out the front door."

"But they'll see us."

"They're going to see us anyway, so we might as well let them see what we want them to see. Make yourselves look like teenagers."

"We are teenagers," Howard says.

"Scared teenagers," I say.

"We are scared teenagers," he says.

"Howard—"

"Okay, I know what you mean."

I lead them forward and slip into character at the same time, swiveling my head from side to side like a confused kid who doesn't know where he's going.

We turn the corner to find two guards with weapons drawn. They stare at us, surprised.

"Stop! Don't move!" the taller one says.

I freeze. Howard and Tanya follow my lead.

I hold out the security card. "My dad says we have to evacuate."

"Your dad?" the guard asks.

He lowers his gun. He steps forward cautiously, hand reaching for the pass. He doesn't touch it, doesn't come any closer than he has to. Instead, he gestures for me to hold the card out farther so he can see it.

He cranes his neck, examining the pass. It's legit.

"I'm Joshua Silberstein," I say. "My dad was giving us a tour. I have to do a report for school."

He looks from me to Howard and Tanya, surprised to discover three frightened kids in the hallway.

The guard holsters his gun.

"Of all the days," he says, rolling his eyes.

He points down the hall. "Keep going this direction. Two rights and a left. I'll let them know you're coming."

"Thanks!" I say.

He speaks into his radio. "Three kids coming out F-1," he says.

"Kids?" the voice replies over the radio.

"Get them the hell out of here before we have a lawsuit on our hands."

When we get to the exit door, there's a group of three guards blocking it. They quickly wave us through.

"I don't know how you kids got in here," the lead guard says.

I shake my head, like I'm as confused as he is.

I see him eyeing Tanya, and I note her head is slightly bowed, her posture meek.

"Are you all right, honey?" he asks.

"I guess," she says.

He pats her on the shoulder as she passes by. It's patronizing. And it gets us through the checkpoint.

Tanya was right. It's easier with her along.

Howard turns the exit door handle, and it opens. He steps outside.

A radio crackles behind me. The lead guard slaps the chest of the guard next to him, bringing him to attention. He points at us.

"*Stop!*" the guard shouts, and the men rush toward us.

Tanya shifts into a defensive stance, preparing to take them on with me. But Howard is outside right now, unprotected.

"Get to the car!" I say, and I push Tanya through the exit door, slamming it tight behind her.

I turn to face the threat alone.

The first guard has a stun gun in his hands. When he lunges at me, I sidestep and grab him, using my better position and leverage to swing his body around. I use his arm like it's my own, delivering a stun charge in the neck of the guard next to him, before spinning and delivering the same charge to his own neck.

Both men fall to the ground, out cold.

One guard remains. A young guy.

He does not go for his stun gun or his radio. He snaps his arm down, and an extendable baton drops out from his wrist. It whips through the air with a whistle. He strikes high, toward my head. I can tell he is nervous and wants this to be over quickly.

I want the same thing. I suspect we're both going to get what we want.

When he comes for my head, I quickly lean backward from the waist. The baton flies past my face, missing my nose by less than half an inch.

His move has thrown him off balance. He's put everything he has into knocking me out in a single blow. It's a rookie move, like a baseball player who tries too hard to hit the first pitch.

It's easy enough for me to step in, swing him over my hip, and throw him to the ground.

"Stop fighting," I say.

If he were smart enough to take my advice, this would be over easily. But he's a fighter, or thinks he is.

He attempts to swing the baton around and catch me across the back. I stamp down hard on the baton, hear it crash to the ground and roll across the hallway. Then I throw an elbow at his head. The impact is enough to knock him senseless.

So much for fighting back.

I hear more guards coming down the hallway.

It's time for me to go. I slam open the door and emerge into the bright sunlight of the parking lot.

TANYA HAS PULLED THE CAR UP TO THE DOOR.

She's in the driver's seat and Howard is next to her.

"Get in," she says, indicating the back.

"Do you know how to drive?" I say.

"Did you seriously just ask me that?"

I climb in.

Tires squeal as Tanya guns the engine, spinning the Accord in a 180-degree arc in the parking lot, until it's dead aimed for the front gate.

She jams the accelerator and makes a run for the exit. Before we can get out, a cloud of dust rises from the road in front of the institute, and a large black Yukon rams the wooden barrier at the front gate as the guards scurry to safety.

The Yukon stops just inside the facility, blocking the only exit.

Tanya slams on the brakes, and we skid to a stop a hundred feet away, facing the gate, head-to-head with the Yukon.

The Yukon's engine revs hard, a V-8 roar that rumbles across the parking lot.

"Who the hell is that?" Howard says.

"Mike," I say.

"That son of a bitch," Tanya says. She says it as if she knows him.

"What do we do?" Howard says.

"We take him on," Tanya says.

"His vehicle outweighs ours by about a ton," I say.

"That just means we're more agile."

She revs the Honda's engine.

"You sure you don't want me to drive?" I say.

"Not a chance," she says.

She pops us into gear, roaring toward the Yukon. Mike does the same, racing forward toward a head-on collision.

"You can't knock him out like this," I say.

"I know what I can and can't do," she says, annoyed with me.

She doesn't flinch, heading straight at Mike as he does the same.

I make sure my seat belt is buckled and I brace for impact. Howard screams—

Tanya swerves hard at the last second, and the front end of the Yukon misses our rear bumper by inches.

Mike roars by, smoke pouring from his wheel wells when he realizes he's missed. He tries to bring the big truck around.

Tanya has a clear shot to the exit now, but she doesn't take it. She turns in the opposite direction, back toward the Yukon.

"What the hell are you doing?" I ask.

"We have to cripple him."

"What if *he* cripples *us*?" Howard says.

"Unlikely," she says, her voice cool.

She weaves forward in a tight serpentine pattern. Mike comes at us, trying to match Tanya's moves, but the physics of his heavy vehicle don't allow him to drive in the same way. His speed drops as he loses forward momentum. Tanya guns the engine and turns hard at the last moment, and our rear bumper clips the front wheel of the Yukon, shredding it to pieces. Shards of metal and rubber fly into the air, and an enormous hubcap rolls past us across the parking lot.

"I guess the second time's the charm," she says, pleased with herself.

"I'm guessing you two have history," I say.

"Everyone has history with Mike," she says.

I want to ask more, but I drop it for the time being.

With Mike's Yukon crippled behind us, Tanya drives unhindered through the front gate. She pulls out of the research institute and swerves onto the open road.

We are free.

TANYA DRIVES LIKE A WOMAN ON A MISSION.

She pushes the Accord hard, getting us to the interstate ramp fast. Right now, it's critical that we put as much distance between ourselves and the institute as possible, so she makes the same short-term gambit I would make, accelerating past sixty, seventy, eighty miles per hour.

"We're going to get pulled over," Howard says. He's hanging on to his seat belt for dear life.

Tanya doesn't answer, all her focus on the road.

We break a hundred miles per hour and keep going, the car shuddering as the metal is stressed by g-forces. I'm most concerned about the rear of the vehicle, where we collided with the Yukon. If there's any internal damage to the structure, this speed could shake us apart.

Tanya must be aware of that, but it's not stopping her.

At this rate, she's putting almost two miles between us and the institute every minute. She risks it for twelve minutes by the clock, a burst that puts us nearly twenty-five miles away. Then she quickly gets off the highway, slowing down to the speed limit.

I watch for chase cars behind us, and I roll down the window and listen for aerial surveillance. I imagine the search grid The Program will create, a map with the institute at the center, concentric circles extending out in ever-widening zones, each of which will be thoroughly investigated. How long before we are caught in one of those zones?

"We have to get rid of this car," I say.

It's badly banged up after our run-in with Mike, and easily identifiable to anyone who might be looking for us.

"There's a truck stop ahead," she says.

When we get there, she pulls around back to the employee parking area.

I know what Tanya is thinking. People tend to stay at truck stops for less than thirty minutes, which means if you steal a car from a truck stop, it's likely to be reported quickly. But if you steal a car from an employee with an eight- to twelve-hour shift, you buy yourself some time.

Tanya stops the Accord and gets out.

"Stay in the car," I tell Howard. "I have to talk to Tanya alone."

Tanya's waiting for me. We face off in the parking lot, eyeing each other warily.

"I'm no danger to you," she says.

"Like you were no danger to Silberstein?"

"He threatened the mission," she says.

"What is your mission, Tanya?"

"What's going on?" Howard asks as he steps out of the car.

"I told you to stay put," I say.

"To hell with that," he says.

He looks back and forth from Tanya to me.

"Why are you two acting so weird?"

"Tanya isn't who she says she is," I tell Howard.

"Who is she?" he asks.

"I work for The Program," Tanya says.

"Work for?" he says.

"I'm an agent."

Howard blinks hard, trying to understand.

"She's an assassin," I say.

Howard's face tells the story. Surprise, upset, betrayal—all at the same time. The poor guy would make a terrible poker player.

Howard says, "But we were prisoners in the house—"

"Tell him the truth," I say. "You owe him that much."

"The Program sent me into the room with you," Tanya says. "They couldn't break you during the interrogation, so they assigned me to befriend you and get you to tell me what you knew."

"So we're not really friends?" Howard says.

Tanya looks upset. It's not easy to disappoint Howard. He's so earnest, it's like kicking a puppy.

"I was doing a job," Tanya says. "I didn't plan on our becoming real friends."

Howard smiles wide. "So we are friends. For real."

"For real," she says.

It looks like Tanya is sincere, but she's fooled me before. I can't let it happen again.

"Are you the Delta agent?" I ask.

"I'm the Gamma," Tanya says.

Francisco told me about the existence of the assassins before I killed him on my last mission. Four agents other than myself. Only three of whom I've met.

I see the org chart in my head:

Mike	Alpha
~~Francisco~~	~~Beta~~
Tanya	Gamma
?	Delta
Me	Epsilon

If Tanya is the Gamma, that would make her a few years older than me.

I say, "You're too young to be the Gamma."

"I'm fifteen. I started The Program much younger than you."

"I understand why you were put in with Howard," I say. "But what happened after?"

"I had no idea who you were when you walked in, Zach. Not until you faced off against Mike. Then it became obvious that you were trained like me."

"But you came with us after that. Why?"

"Howard was my mark. You stay with the mark until your orders change."

"You said your orders were to find out what Howard knew and whether he was connected to me. Once you knew the truth, you should have terminated us. But you helped us instead. Why?"

"I don't know," she says.

"Have you spoken to Mother?" I ask.

"Yes."

"When you called your grandmother on my phone?"

"That's right. It was an emergency protocol. I let Mother know that I was safe and with Howard. But no more."

"You didn't tell her about me?" I say.

"No."

And Mike wouldn't have told her anything, because to do so would raise questions about what he was doing there in the first place.

"Which brings us back to my first question. Why?"

"Maybe I'm confused," she says.

I look at Tanya, deciding my next move.

I still have Silberstein's gun in my waistband. I could take Tanya out into the field beyond the parking lot, away from the restaurant where people might hear a gunshot. I could make it look like an assault gone awry. An underage runaway hanging out at a truck stop meets the wrong person. Tragedy ensues.

"You're planning to get rid of me," Tanya says.

"How do you know?" I ask.

"That's what I would be doing right now."

"Stop it, both of you," Howard says. "I got the info about your father, Zach. Can't we just leave her here?"

I glance over at him and see that he's holding out the thumb drive. Howard's uncomfortable, and I don't blame him. He's not trained to deal with situations like this.

But I am.

"We can't let her go," I say quietly. "She's seen us. Which means we're not safe."

Howard stares at the ground, afraid to meet my eye.

Tanya takes a step toward me. I reach for the gun in my waistband.

"You don't need the gun," she says.

"I'll decide that for myself," I say.

She shrugs. "You're going to do what you're going to do, Zach. But before you kill me, I have to tell you something."

I nod, fully expecting her to plead for her life.

"It's about your father," she says. "He's alive."

ALIVE.

For a moment I feel unsteady on my feet.

"I don't believe you," I say. "You'll tell me anything right now to save yourself."

"I don't want to die," she says. "But I'm not going to lie to you. I'll tell you what you need to know, and then you can decide what you want to do with me."

"Talk," I say. "I'll listen."

"Your father is alive and working for The Program. That's why Howard found those e-mails. You remember how Silberstein said The Program wanted to take over their research?"

"He said my father refused. That's why they killed him."

"That's what he believed, but it's a lie. The Program didn't just take their research, they took your father to run it, too."

"Why lie to Silberstein?"

"He was deemed a security risk, so they kept him on the science side of things and walled him off from the military applications."

"And his story?"

"Everyone has a different story about your father. You know how

The Program works. It's a Chinese box, stories nested in stories behind other stories. Nobody gets the full truth. Mother makes sure of it."

"You're saying that you know the full truth?"

"I know enough of it to help you. There may be more that I don't know."

"But you can tell me for sure that my father is alive? Why would I believe you?"

"The accident they staged on the bridge. Your father's body was not in that car."

"You have proof?" I ask.

"I don't need proof. I was there."

Howard gasps, but I'm not buying her story.

"It was nearly five years ago," I say. "You couldn't have been there."

"Pull up the article from the newspaper," Tanya says. "The one we were looking at earlier."

I take my phone and toss it to Howard. He finds the article and tosses the phone back.

"Check out the second picture," she says. "The one taken at the scene of the accident."

I scroll down. A group of townspeople stands on the bridge, staring at the place where the car went off the road. There are children there, one in particular who is pointing toward the break in the railing.

"Look at the girl who's pointing," Tanya says.

There's a photo of a young girl, maybe ten years old, wearing a cap. I pinch out and magnify the image on the screen. I look at the girl's eyes, the shape of her nose in relation to her brow—

I compare that face with Tanya's.

"The little girl is you," I say to her.

I toss the phone back to Howard.

He looks at the picture on the phone, then at Tanya, then back to the phone.

"Oh my God," he says.

"I was ten years old," Tanya says. "My first year in The Program and one of my earliest assignments. I was planted in town as the daughter of a couple on vacation for the summer. I was told to ride my bike out by the bridge at a certain time so I could witness the accident and call the police. I was there when they arrived, while they investigated, and when the reporters got to the scene. What's more credible than an innocent child pointing for the camera?"

It sounds exactly like a Program operation.

"There were bodies in the car, Zach, but they weren't your parents. Silberstein didn't know that. They wanted him to think it was an accident, because that would neutralize his doubts and shore up the story for anyone who worked with your father."

"So my father wasn't in the car?" I ask.

She shakes her head. "I met him later that week. Mother introduced me."

I'm trying to process what I'm hearing, but it's more difficult than I expected. Normally I can take in information and sort it instantly, but when it comes to my own family, my thinking is cloudy.

"My father would never work for The Program," I say.

"He would if he had no choice," Tanya says.

"What do you mean?"

"Isn't it obvious?" she says. "He had to work for them because they took his son."

Howard and I exchange looks.

"You're their bargaining chip," Tanya says. "Your father can't rebel as long as he knows your life is on the line. At least that's how it was explained to me."

I think of my father that last time I saw him, tied up and bleeding in the chair in our living room. Mike drugged me and took me into the room before I passed out.

It all makes sense now.

Mike took me in, not so I could see my father, but so my father could see me.

I'm thinking about that time now, lost in the memory, when a buzzing sound pulls me back to the present.

Howard is saying my name. He's holding out my phone.

"Someone is calling," he says.

I look at the phone.

"It's Mother," I say.

"I told you the truth earlier," Tanya says. "She doesn't know we're together, but by now, she has to suspect you. Play along. Convince her everything is fine, and you'll get closer to your father."

I look at Tanya, then down at my phone where Mother's ID code is flashing on the screen.

If Tanya is telling the truth, that means my father is alive. And The Program has him.

It takes everything I have to center myself, remove any trace of upset from my face and voice.

Then I answer the phone.

MOTHER LOOKS OUT AT ME FROM THE IPHONE SCREEN.

"It's been too long since we've seen each other," Mother says.

Her voice is uncharacteristically warm.

"We spoke yesterday, Mother. Don't you remember?"

"Of course I do. I meant since I've seen you in person, Zach."

The comment surprises me. We do not see each other in person anymore. I haven't been in the same space as her since graduation nearly five years ago.

"No more missions. I want you to come home," Mother says.

I feel the muscles in my face tense.

Mother has thrown communication protocols out the window. She's used my name, she's talking about real issues. This is unprecedented.

I keep my breathing steady, return my attention to the phone.

"Why now?" I say.

"You've got a birthday coming up," Mother says.

"Do I?"

"Now you're the one who doesn't remember."

I break protocol and say, *"Birthdays are remnants of a life that no longer exists.* It's you who taught me that while I was training."

"At the time, I was trying to protect you."

"And now?"

"Nothing has changed. I'm still trying to protect you," she says.

My senses are on high alert, warning signals buzzing in my head.

"I don't need hand-holding," I say.

"Nobody said you did. But even soldiers get leave. They relax and recuperate before heading back into battle."

It's true. Nobody can fight forever.

"Come home," Mother says. "We'll celebrate your birthday together."

Two possibilities that I can see:

One, Mother knows exactly what happened at the holding house. She knows I was there, and she may know where I am now. If that's the case, this is a trap.

Two, Mother suspects but doesn't know. This offer is meant to bring me close so she can find out the truth.

Then a third possibility occurs to me. What if the offer is legit?

"What do you say?" Mother asks.

I have to make a choice.

A month ago I wanted this, so I will want it now.

"A birthday party? Sounds like fun," I say.

"Anything you want for a gift?"

"Cash is always nice."

Mother smiles and her energy lightens.

"I'll see what I can do," she says.

I glance at Tanya. She nods, silently urging me on.

Mother says, "I'm pinging your phone with a meet-up location. We will be there at dusk to pick you up."

"You mean tonight?"

"You should be able to get to the location with time to spare. The instructions will be encoded in the ping."

"Simple," I say.

"Zach, I wasn't lying when I said you were my favorite. Nobody has accomplished the things you have, and in such a short period of time. You are very special."

I smile, acknowledging the compliment.

"I'll see you soon, Mom."

"You will," she says, and the call ends.

A moment later the ping arrives. I decode it, and a tag appears in a rural area of Pennsylvania near the Buchanan State Forest. That's where the pickup will happen.

"When and where?" Tanya says.

"A few hours from now in Pennsylvania."

"Are you going to do it?" Howard says.

"You have to do it," Tanya says. "If you want to find your real father."

Is it a trap?

I think back to what Mike said in the coffee shop. The Program is not familiar with insubordination. I see now that he was telling the truth. The Program is confused about me, and they don't yet know if there's a connection between Howard and me.

"Can you get there in time?" Howard says.

"If I hurry. Mother thinks I'm coming from Columbus, Ohio. We're about the same distance from the pickup point, just in the opposite direction."

I look at Tanya.

What am I going to do about her?

"Zach, can I talk to you for a minute alone?" Howard says.

"Now? Are you serious?"

"It's important," he says.

I motion for Howard to come closer to me. I watch Tanya over his shoulder, looking for any sign of movement toward us.

"What about Tanya?" he whispers.

"You can't trust anything she's said to you. She's trained to play a role."

"What role is she playing right now?" he says.

I glance back at her.

"I don't know. That's what troubles me."

"If she wanted to stop us, she could have done it already. Plus, she saved me from Silberstein. Don't forget that."

"Do you really think Silberstein was going to shoot you?"

"It seemed like it. He was freaking out, waving the gun around, shouting for me to get away from the computer."

Howard seems convinced of what he saw.

"Listen, Howard, I know you like her—"

"You like her, too," he says.

I pause, frustrated.

"I want you to consider something," I say. "When the two of you met, it was under extreme duress. There's a phenomenon called trauma bonding—"

"Shut up," he says, his face red with anger.

"You've been traumatized," I say. "I think it's affecting your judgment."

"What about you? You've been traumatized, too. Have you thought about that?"

"I'm not traumatized."

"You killed Lee and his sister not too long ago. You killed Samara in New York. How many bodies were there before I met you?"

The faces of my targets appear in my mind, flipping over like playing cards.

"It's my job," I say. "I'm trained to deal with these things. They don't bother me."

Howard shakes his head. "I don't believe that," he says.

The wind picks up, whistling between the Dumpsters. It catches an empty can and sends it rolling across the dirt.

"You have feelings, Zach. I know you do."

"You're wrong about that."

"I don't think so."

"You want me to let Tanya go? Is that what this is all about?"

"I want her to come with us. At least until we find out whose side she's really on."

"She can kill you."

"She hasn't killed me yet."

I look at Tanya across the parking lot. She's looking at the ground like someone pretending not to pay attention while her best friends fight.

I think about the possibility of taking her with us. On one hand, it's absurd. But what is the alternative? If I leave her here, she can give us away to The Program.

Howard may be right. It's safer to have her with us.

"We're leaving now," I say.

"We?" Tanya says. She looks at me expectantly.

"Together," I say.

Howard smiles. "This is awesome," he says.

Tanya smiles, too. "Thank you, Zach."

"We have to get to the pickup point before sundown," I say. "No time for a celebration."

"We should ditch this Accord," Howard says. He looks around

the parking lot, his gaze falling on a little Civic that's been tricked out, double exhausts poking out the back.

"How about that one?" he says.

"I think you like Japanese cars," Tanya says.

"His girlfriend's Japanese," I say.

Howard blushes.

Then we steal the car.

FIVE HOURS IS A LONG TIME.

A long time to listen to Howard and Tanya talking in the backseat. A long time to hear Tanya singing along with a country station in a sweet, steady voice.

A long time to think about what I'm doing.

Tanya said my father is alive, a prisoner of The Program. If that's true, I have to find him and free him.

Maybe Tanya's right. Instead of moving further from The Program, now is the time to move toward it, to reunite with Mother and play along.

"Did you find anything interesting at the institute?" I ask Howard. "Anything that might give me some insight into where they're keeping my father?"

Howard says, "The computer in Silberstein's lab, it's what's known as a 'thin client.' It's basically just a monitor with access to the server where the real data is kept."

"Like a window of sorts?"

"More like a tunnel. But you get the idea. The security setup is similar to the one I found before, but the data sets are different."

"Different how?"

"The ones I found in New Hampshire were military operations, strategic plans. The stuff at the institute is scientific research, more technical."

"I'm not following you. Was Silberstein working for The Program?"

"Definitely. But I think things are compartmentalized. He's walled off from accessing the military information."

"Chinese boxes," Tanya says. "Like I told you."

Howard reaches into his pocket and removes the thumb drive. "The rest of it is here. I need a computer and several hours to sort through it all."

"We don't have either of those things."

I check the car clock.

"I'm running out of time, Howard. And so are you."

He slumps back in the seat, defeated.

I drive on.

By the time we arrive in southern Pennsylvania, there's less than an hour to spare before sunset.

I steal a glance into the backseat. Tanya and Howard have fallen asleep. I look at Tanya's face, and I think about what's going to happen in a few minutes. I'll get on a helicopter, and she'll be alone with Howard....

I stop on the side of a road about five miles from the pickup point. The motion of the car rocks them awake.

"Are we there?" Howard says.

"Not quite yet," I say. "I have to talk to Tanya."

"Not again," Howard says.

Tanya and I get out and stand in front of the car.

"You're not taking me the rest of the way?" she asks.

"No."

"I think you're making a mistake, Zach. Let me stay with Howard while you go into The Program. I'll keep him safe, and we'll both be waiting for you when you come out."

There's no guarantee that I'll make it out. But I don't broach that subject with her.

I shake my head. "I won't do it," I say.

"You're going to leave him alone out here? That's crazy."

"And leaving him with an assassin makes more sense? He's a lot stronger than he looks. You were with him at the holding house."

"He's strong," she says, "but he's not trained. He won't make it out here. Not if The Program is searching for him."

"Hopefully I'll get back before they can find him."

"Hopefully? You're willing to risk his life on hopefully?"

"I don't have a lot of options."

"Are you going to kill me?"

"I've thought about it."

I note a subtle shift in her stance as she prepares herself.

"Why did you help us, Tanya? At the research facility. And after." She bites her lower lip.

"Like I told you, I had a mission, and I stayed with Howard because he was my mark. But something happened. I started to get...confused."

"About what?" I say.

"Why you'd risk your life for Howard when he's not one of us."

"He's my friend."

"We don't have friends," she says.

"I do."

She stares at me. "How?" she says.

"I deviated from my mission a while ago in New York," I say. "Things started to unravel after that."

"What does that mean, you deviated?"

"I asked questions."

She nods. "I've wanted to ask questions, too."

"Have you ever done it?"

"Not until now."

She sighs and runs her fingers through her hair.

She says, "I understand if you need to—to get rid of me. Just make it quick. You know how to do that."

"I'm not going to kill you," I say. "I'm letting you go."

"How do you know I won't call Mother and give you away?"

"I don't know."

"You're letting me go when I can be a danger to you? It doesn't make sense."

"Earlier you said I should follow my instincts. I'm following them."

"You're taking a big risk."

"I'm trusting you," I say.

"That goes against your training," she says.

"So, we've both gone against our training."

I glance at my phone. Thirty minutes until the pickup, and I still have to drive to the location, get Howard situated, and prepare.

"You'd better get moving," Tanya says.

"Yeah."

"Be careful, Zach."

"Stay safe," I say.

I want to say more, but I don't. I turn and walk back to the car. The engine is still running. I slide into the driver's seat.

"You sent her away," Howard says, hurt in his voice.

"It was the safest choice."

"For who?"

I don't respond. When I look up, Tanya is gone.

I put the car in gear and drive.

I TURN ON MY PROGRAM PHONE.

I disengage the leapfrog app, revealing my true location to The Program. With a pickup minutes away, there's no need to hide anymore.

I use my phone to locate the nearest city that will have a large police force, instructing Howard to make his way there. He'll tell the cops he's a runaway who wants to go home. Once he's in the care of the police, it will be harder for The Program to make a move on him. Howard listens, nodding to show that he understands. He's made it this far, and if his luck holds, he may make it all the way home.

By that time I will be back with The Program, and I may be able to affect the outcome from the inside, steer Program assets away from him or bury his story entirely. I won't know until I get inside and understand the situation from Mother and Father's perspective.

The helicopter passes over the canopy above us.

"That's my ride," I say.

"Good luck," Howard says.

"You too."

"Will I see you again?"

"I don't know," I say.

He steps in and gives me a hug.

This time I hug him back. Hard.

The sound of the rotors changes. The helicopter is hovering over the pickup zone about half a mile away.

I reach into my pocket, withdraw Silberstein's pistol, and offer it to Howard. Howard shrinks back when he sees it.

"For protection," I say.

"I don't need it."

"I want you to carry it until you get to a city. Then throw it in a river or drop it through a sewer grate. Before you do, wipe it down with a soft cloth or a corner of your T-shirt."

"Wipe it for fingerprints," Howard says. "Just like in the movies."

"Rub hard. You're smudging out invisible oils that come from your fingertips."

"I don't really know how to fire a gun," Howard says.

"I showed you once before."

"But I'm not good at it."

"You don't need to be good. Just point it in the right direction and let the gun do the work."

It takes a lot more training than that to properly use a weapon, but in this case it will have to do.

I can see the helicopter over the tree line a little ways from here. I start to move toward it.

"Where will they take you?" Howard calls after me.

I don't know the answer to the question, so I just say, "Home."

I RUN.

Through the woods, up one hill and down another, the thrum of the rotors growing in volume.

I crest the top of another hill and I see the helicopter landing in a small valley with a hill on one side and a river on the other. Together they form a natural defensive perimeter.

I walk down the hill, approaching the aircraft slowly, my hands held away from my body so it's clear I'm not carrying a weapon.

I can make out a pilot in the front seat wearing a helmet with a reflective visor that covers most of his face. There's a copilot in the passenger seat, similarly dressed.

The cargo bay door slides open, and a third man steps out. He wears no helmet.

It's Father, my commander in The Program. He's come for me himself.

I lift a hand in greeting. I walk toward the open door.

"Hello, son," he says, shouting to be heard over the noise of the rotors.

"Another helicopter ride?" I say, referring to our last mission together.

"It's worked for us before. Why mess with success?"

"You want to drive, or you want me to?" I say.

"This time we're both passengers. It will give us a chance to talk."

He extends a hand, pulling me up into the helicopter and sliding the door closed behind us.

The helicopter makes a combat takeoff, rising with maximum power. It's a dangerous maneuver normally undertaken in battle conditions.

"Combat maneuvers?" I say to Father.

"A precaution," Father says.

I'm confused for a moment, wondering what risk there could be in a rural area of Pennsylvania.

That's when I understand.

It's me they're worried about. I am the risk.

I look around the cargo bay. Two soldiers in combat gear flank us. They are armed and in shooting position, ready to attack if called upon.

Father leans in close so he can be heard.

"You'll forgive me if I get right to business," he says.

"Of course."

I relax my shoulders, allowing my body to react as if I'm unconcerned about the weapons being pointed at me.

Father says, "We've had reports of some unusual activity in the last twenty-four hours."

"Could you be more specific?" I say.

"Is that necessary?"

"It is if you want me to know what you're talking about."

Father studies my eyes. I show him nothing.

"We had a security breach at a Program facility," Father says.

"Are you accusing me?" I say.

"I'm asking you."

"I've been standing down in Columbus for several days now. If I recall, it's you who took me off the board in the first place. You said I needed some rest."

"Zach, I'm trying to help you here. I need you to level with me."

Help me with what?

I hesitate for a moment, wondering if there's more going on than I can perceive. Perhaps I should tell Father the truth.

No. This is a game of chess. Move. Countermove.

"Here's the truth," I say. "I was in Columbus. Mother called and asked me to join her for a birthday celebration. I would have brought party favors, but time was a little tight."

"That's all you have to say?"

"That's all there is."

"You don't know anything about these issues I mentioned?"

"I don't."

"And you would tell me if you did."

"What choice would I have?"

Father smiles. "All right, then. That's all I needed to know."

He taps a button on his shoulder and speaks into a throat microphone. I can't hear what he says, but a moment later the helicopter banks left and gains altitude.

"We're on our way," he says.

I relax, settling back into my seat. Father does the same in the seat across from me.

"Can you tell me where we're headed?" I say.

"We want to show you the operation now. You'll be amazed how we've grown since the old days when you first came to us."

"Old days? That was barely five years ago."

"Things change fast," he says. "Sit back and enjoy the ride."

I sense movement from the soldier behind me, but before I can react to the threat, the soldier has sprayed an aerosol gas into my face from a small canister. I can taste the bitterness of the gas in the back of my throat.

I look at Father.

"It's not poison," he says, answering my question before I've asked. "It will help you relax and protect us until we've done a thorough evaluation."

"Protect you?"

"Mother said we should bring you in, but I don't think she's aware of how far you've strayed. I know you're lying to me, so I've decided to undertake a different protocol."

I try to stand, only to find my legs shaky beneath me.

"Don't fight it," Father says.

I'm not fighting. I'm consciously slowing my breathing and my heart rate. A drug is delivered via the bloodstream, and the quicker the blood is moving, the more efficient the delivery. By slowing my heart rate, I can slow the dispersal rate of whatever it is they've used on me.

"Why are you doing this?" I ask.

"Three incidents in the last day. One in our holding house, another at the University of Rochester, and a third at an institute with which we are affiliated. These are not coincidences. There are no coincidences when you're involved."

"I told you I don't know anything about it."

"If that's true, then you have nothing to worry about," Father says. "I'll ask you a few questions, and we'll be done. When I'm satisfied, I'll take you to Mother."

The drug is entering my system. I feel my mental faculties slowing, my breathing becoming labored.

"Did you snatch that kid from the house?" Father says.

"What kid?"

"The boy we found in your hotel room in New Hampshire."

He's talking about Howard.

My first option is to say nothing at all. Ride out the interrogation.

The other option is to tell the truth—let Father know I took Howard, and explain the reasons behind my actions.

For now I will make the choice that buys Howard the most time to get away.

"I don't know anything about a kid," I say.

"We'll find out," Father says. "One way or another."

A thick nylon belt slips over my head, constricting against my chest. It's the soldier behind me. He pulls on the belt, attempting to bind me to the seat.

Under normal circumstances, I would have sensed it coming and evaded, but the drug is slowing my reaction time.

I have to play defense. I get my forearm up between my body and the belt, exerting pressure to try to break free.

"Don't fight it," Father says again.

But I am fighting now, even as the drug's effects are increasing with each passing moment.

Father tries to push me back into the seat as the soldier behind me pulls on the belt, but I resist them both, the tension in the belt growing tighter as I exert my full strength against it.

The chopper angles left, and Father stumbles and falls to the deck. I steal a look around, assessing my strategic position.

Father is on the floor across from me, his eyes wide with surprise. The soldier is still behind me, yanking on the belt. The two pilots are up front, not yet aware of any problem in the helicopter bay. The third soldier comes into view in my peripheral vision, stepping forward to help his comrade.

"Stop this, Zach," Father says.

But I don't stop. I fight harder, anger growing inside me. I think of how Mother wasn't willing to bring me in after the Natick mission, then how she and Father changed my target in New York, sending me after Samara. The anger fuels me, and I make one last effort to overpower the soldier behind me. I heave forward with all my weight, and he loses his footing, flying past me across the cabin and crashing into Father.

That's when the operative in my peripheral vision brings up his weapon to fire.

"No," Father shouts, but the command is lost in the roar of the chopper blades as the soldier pulls the trigger.

I kick out at the gun, my heel making contact with the inside of the soldier's wrist.

Instead of letting go, he hangs on and depresses the trigger. Three shots spray out. The flash of the muzzle is temporarily blinding in the dark of the helicopter bay.

The soldier leaps forward to tackle me, and suddenly the helicopter angles to the side, hard. I glance forward and see the pilot slumped over in his seat, his brain splattered against the front windscreen, the electronics sparking in the instrument panel.

The pilot is dead, and the copilot is fighting to regain control.

Suddenly the cargo bay door slides open, wind buffeting the inside of the helicopter.

It's the soldier who was behind me. Maybe he's planning to push me outside, get rid of the problem once and for all.

I grab some rope dangling above my head and kick out at him. The soldier goes through the open door instead of me, his arms windmilling as he flies out into the darkness.

I try to locate Father and see he's been thrown all the way to the back of the helicopter, where he's tangled up in cargo netting. He's fighting to get free, but the helicopter is rolling on its side now, flinging the other soldier head over limb through the cabin. I grab at a wall handle to prevent myself from joining him. If I can claw my way to the pilot's seat, I might have a chance to stabilize—

It's too late.

The helicopter passes the critical angle where the rotor loses its grip on the air, and we turn like a ship keeling over in the water, rolling until we are upside down and falling out of the sky.

The open door is below me. I can jump and take my chances, or I can ride the bird to the ground. It's almost always better to stay in a vehicle during a crash. The metal structure absorbs the bulk of the impact much better than human flesh. Usually. Not always.

The helicopter is still spinning and falling, the floor briefly under my feet rather than over my head. The open door is in front of me.

Stay or go? I have to decide before gravity decides for me.

I look back at Father. He's scrambling to buckle himself into a crash seat. He shouts for me to do the same, pointing to the seat next to him. I can barely hear him over the sound of the warning alarms.

Join Father or jump?

I leap for the open door, spreading my arms to create some wind resistance as the helicopter spins down and away from me.

I relax my body as I fall. I try to flow with the impact, curling into a ball and letting inertia carry me, keeping my limbs tucked and hoping to limit the damage to my frame.

I feel myself hit and roll down the hill, my skin tearing from friction, my body moving so fast that it feels like it will never stop.

I finally come to rest in the tall grass on the banks of a river.

A hundred yards behind me, I hear the sickening crunch of metal as the helicopter smashes into the ground.

I press my face into the earth, making myself as small a target as possible. Shards of metal whiz by above my head as the helicopter rotors break up on impact. Chunks of earth fall around me.

Eventually the noise stops, replaced by the sound of the river flowing in front of me. I crawl forward and bring my lips to the water.

The drug is coursing through my system now, mitigated only by the intense adrenaline rush of the crash and fall. I dunk my head in the water, trying to stay awake, but already I am fading, the drug carrying me out of this world and into unconsciousness.

I slap at my face, forcing my eyes open. I sit up, wincing from the pain, and look behind me. The wrecked carcass of the helicopter is pressed into the side of a hill, smoke drifting in thick trails above it. The once open door is crumpled and half the roof is torn off. I can barely see the outline of bodies inside.

I stand on unsteady legs and stumble toward the wreckage, trying to make out images through the smoke. One soldier lies across the ground with his chest torn open, blood and flesh spilling out. The copilot's torso has been forced through the shattered windscreen, his body wrecked.

I move closer still.

Inside the helicopter bay, I see a dangling arm attached to a limp body.

Father.

He's buckled into his seat, but the helicopter is on its side, and the seat is high up in the air.

His arm moves. He is alive.

The acrid smell of aviation fuel fills my nose.

A fire has started on the other side of the helicopter. It spreads from the ground where the earth is soaked through with fuel. With a whooshing sound, the area around the helicopter catches flame.

I look to Father, his arm moving more frantically now.

He is struggling in his seat, fighting to unlatch his belt and get himself out of the wreckage. But an interior brace has fallen and covered his body, pinning him back into the seat. He cannot reach the latch.

I stumble toward him.

There is a loud popping sound and the flames rise up the sides of the helicopter.

I try to speed up, but the drug is hitting me hard. My vision grays out at the edges. My feet seem to belong to someone else.

I get within twenty feet of the helicopter, but the flames are licking up the sides and rolling along the top, engulfing the entire craft, moving toward the fuel tank. I know what's going to happen, but I'm powerless to stop it, unable to get there in time.

Father knows what's about to happen, too, because his clawing motion stops. His body grows still.

I look in and see his face lit by flames.

He is awake and looking back at me.

I was trained to call this man Father, but he was never my father. He was my commander. If we had gotten to our destination, he would have become my interrogator.

He has been other things as well. My savior. My mentor.

Much has passed between us, good and bad. My feelings about him are complex, but I would save him now if I could.

Maybe he knows this. Our eyes meet, and he appears to be smiling at me.

It's a generous smile, almost like forgiveness.

Then the helicopter explodes, blowing me to the ground and pulling me into an inky blackness that is not sleep, not death, but something in between.

MY EYES ARE OPEN.

But I do not remember opening them.

The moon is bright above me. I am moving slowly across the grass, but not under my own power.

How is that possible?

It takes me a few moments to put it together.

I'm being dragged, my arms above my head, Howard grasping my wrists as he pulls me away from the crash.

I try to speak, but my mouth does not work. I cannot control the muscles of my lips.

I gasp for air. I feel my eyes roll into the back of my head.

"Something's wrong," I hear Howard say.

Who is he talking to?

I cannot feel my body, but I sense something bad is happening. The oxygen is not flowing to my brain.

I must have stopped breathing. I should be afraid, but I am not. Is my neurosuppressor so effective in its design that I can watch myself die without fear?

"What do we do?" I hear Howard say.

His voice has the panicked edge that my own thoughts do not.

"Can you hear me, Zach?" Tanya's voice now.

My body stops moving as her face appears above mine.

What is Tanya doing here?

"Zach?" she says.

I cannot answer her. I can only look at her eyes, noting how beautiful they are. The fact surprises me, as if I've never really looked at her before.

She kneels next to me. She slaps at my face, but there is no pain.

"Stay with me," she says.

I want to. I can't.

She slaps again.

I think of Samara on the ground in Central Park, looking up at me after I injected her with poison.

It doesn't hurt, she said.

"Zach," Tanya shouts again, her voice upset.

It doesn't hurt, I try to tell her, but I cannot form the words.

Tanya's face comes close to mine. I remember a lesson from my training: It is dangerous to let people get too close to you. They can harm you when they are close.

Tanya presses her lips to mine.

Why is she kissing me?

The light of the moon grows brighter. The hazy thoughts gain focus.

Tanya lifts her head, takes a breath, and kisses me again.

That's when I understand that she isn't kissing me. She's performing mouth-to-mouth resuscitation.

The realization is funny to me, but I cannot laugh.

I can only lie there, unmoving, while her lips bring me back to life.

I DO NOT DREAM.

I float in darkness for an undetermined amount of time. Eventually a light in my eyes awakens me. Only then do I realize I've been sleeping.

I'm looking at a painted white ceiling above my head, a light fixture with a ceiling fan slowly whirring. It's a decorative fan, one you'd find in someone's home.

What am I doing in a home?

I look to the side of the bed.

Tanya is there, holding my hand. Or so it seems for a second until I realize she's checking my pulse. She glances up at me, startled to find me awake.

"You're back," she says.

"How long was I out?" I try to sit up, but the room spins.

"Easy," she says, propping up pillows behind me.

"How long?"

"All night. It's morning now."

I look out the window. The sun is bright. Midmorning.

"Where are we?" I say.

"A house. It was empty. We broke in."

"No alarms?"

"Howard checked. We've been here all night without a problem."

"You're awake," Howard says, appearing in the doorway. I'm surprised by how much of a relief it is to see him.

"Are you feeling okay?" I say.

"I'm good," he says, "but I'm not the one who survived a helicopter crash."

The crash. It comes back to me in a series of flashes. The struggle inside the helicopter, the violence of impact, followed by the flames. I see a man smiling at me.

Father.

"Did anyone else make it?" I ask.

Howard shakes his head. "No," he says. "Only you."

"We have to get out of here," I say, trying to sit up.

Again, Tanya puts out a hand to stop me. "Slow down," she says.

"You don't understand," I say.

"I understand very well," she says. "I was there, Zach."

"How?"

"I followed you through the woods to the pickup point."

"We drove to the pickup point. It was five miles."

"You haven't seen me run yet," she says. "You don't know how fast I am."

"You saw the crash?"

"And I saw Father," she says.

"Who?" Howard says.

"One of the men who died. We call him Father," Tanya says. "He is second in command of The Program. *Was*, I should say."

I monitor her face, trying to understand her reaction. Our commander was killed because of me. What is she going to do about it?

"They'll be looking for us now," I say.

"They've been looking all along," Tanya says.

"Not like they will now. You know what I mean."

"We're far away from the crash," Howard says.

"How far?"

"Twenty miles," Tanya says.

"You dragged me for twenty miles?"

"We got a ride."

"Shit."

"It was a trucker," Howard says. "Big rig. Tanya told him you were drunk and we needed a ride. He drove us, dropped us off nearby, then kept going."

"They'll find the trucker," I say.

"He said he was headed for New Orleans," Howard says.

"It's only a matter of time," I say.

"Tanya searched the area and found this summer house that had already been closed up for the season. Wi-Fi and cable are turned off. Electricity and water are fine."

"I've been watching for activity outside," Tanya says. "Nothing unusual."

"Nothing you can see. But they might have drones."

"Are you injured?" Howard says.

I do a quick scan of my body, head to toe and back again. I flex muscle groups, move my joints. My body aches, but I'm functional. My head is another matter. I have a headache and double vision.

"I've got a mild concussion," I say. "But I've had a lot worse."

My mind is racing as I think about what The Program will do now. They may know I was on board the helicopter, or they may not. The crash is likely to have confused the issue. Bodies burned beyond recognition, an explosion that spreads the remains. It will take time to sort through all of it, to test the DNA and determine if anyone got away.

I think about the moments after the explosion. The image of Howard dragging me across the grass.

"You saved me," I say to Howard.

"I helped," he says. "But I think she was the one who saved you."

He points to Tanya.

Then I remember. Tanya hovering over me, giving me mouth-to-mouth.

I reach out and touch her arm.

"Thank you," I say.

Her skin is warm. It feels good to touch her.

I take my hand away.

"I wish I needed mouth-to-mouth," Howard says.

He's jealous.

Tanya feels it, too. "It's not like we kissed," she says. "It was medical attention."

"Whatever," Howard says. I can sense that he's upset, but there isn't time to discuss it now.

"Pack everything and let's get ready to leave," I say.

I crawl out of bed, and I almost fall. Tanya steadies me.

"Let's talk about this," she says. "You need rest, and your body needs time to heal."

"We don't have time," I say.

Tanya considers the situation. "You think we should move on?" she asks.

"I think it would be best."

She pauses, mulling over the scenario just as I would do.

After a moment she nods. "Okay, then. There's a Jeep in the garage. Keys above the driver's visor and a full tank of gas."

"You prepped it?"

"Prepped and ready to roll."

"Nice work," I say.

"I kept myself busy while you were passed out." She turns to Howard. "Fill the back of the Jeep with as much food as you can. Dry goods preferred, things that will last without refrigeration."

"Okay. What are you going to do?" Howard says.

"I'm going to take a shower," Tanya says. "I'm disgusting."

"Women," Howard says, shaking his head.

"You smell pretty bad, too," Tanya says to him. "We're going to be in that Jeep for a while."

Howard sniffs at his shirt.

"It's a fifty-percenter," he says.

"What's a fifty-percenter?" Tanya asks.

"It's how I smell when I'm halfway through a hacking marathon."

"How about everyone does what they need to do and we get the hell out of here?" I say.

They nod. Howard leaves the room and Tanya follows.

I take a few moments to stretch and gauge my strength. I flex my legs. I clench my fists, checking the power in my grip.

I turn to find Tanya standing in the doorway watching me.

"For real," she says. "Are you okay?"

I crane my neck, bounce up and down on the balls of my feet.

"Seem to be," I say.

"I don't mean physically," she says. "I saw what happened to Father."

"He's not my real father. Or yours."

"He was still important to you. To us."

"Are you angry?" I say.

"Yes. But I'm other things, too."

"Like what?"

"Relieved."

She studies my face.

"Are you surprised by that?" she asks.

"I am."

"Like I said earlier, I've had my own issues with The Program," she says. "At first, the idea of carrying out missions without knowing why was easy. No information meant no reason for doubt. But a few years in, I started to wonder why I was doing it. That's when the questions began."

"Sounds familiar."

"And it's not like there's a Q&A session after each mission."

"Not yet. But I put it in the suggestion box, so you never know."

She laughs. Then she says, "I noticed you didn't answer my question about Father."

Her eyes are gentle. She's not angry, only trying to talk to me about what happened.

"It's not a big deal," I say.

"I don't believe you," she says.

"Maybe I don't want to talk about it."

She nods. But she still doesn't leave.

"I'm a lot like you," she says.

"How's that?"

"I keep it all inside. Or I used to. It's different now."

"I don't know what you mean."

She lowers her voice. "Without the chip," she says.

"You know about the chip?"

"I had a first gen. It was removed when the upgrade became available."

"I didn't know there were different versions," I say.

"They keep innovating. But I never got the upgrade."

"Why not?"

"It turns out that I'm more effective without it. At least on my particular kinds of missions."

"What are your missions?"

"They're more—I guess you'd say—emotional in nature."

"You're a chameleon."

"We're all chameleons," she says. "But I have to do things that you don't have to do."

"Things?"

"Relationships. Sex."

"Because you're a woman."

I see a flash of pain behind her eyes.

"We've all done things we didn't want to do," I say.

"I believe that," she says.

She steps toward me.

"What about now?" she asks. She reaches up and puts a hand on my chest. "Is this something you don't want to do?"

"That depends what we're doing."

She leans in and kisses me.

"Does that answer your question?" she says.

"One of them."

"You have more? Go ahead and ask."

"All right," I say. "Am I kissing you or am I kissing an assassin?"

"Maybe a little of both. You want to search me again? For your own safety?"

"That sounds like a good idea," I say.

We reach for each other, and the talking stops.

WE LIE IN BED AFTER, WRAPPED IN EACH OTHER'S ARMS.

Tanya traces the scar on my chest, running a finger over the mark between my pec and my shoulder.

"Can I ask you a question?" she says.

"It's a knife scar," I say.

Graduation day. My first real fight with Mike.

"I don't care about the scar," she says. "It's a different question. I want to know what happened to you."

"I don't understand."

"How is it possible for you to go against orders? I'm trained just like you. I know what you've been taught and how powerful that teaching is."

"It didn't happen all at once. A series of missions, a series of questions. Looking back, I can see that the questions were always there. I just ignored them for a long time. Eventually, I guess, they got too loud to ignore."

I stroke the soft skin on the side of her cheek and down her neck. She shivers under my fingers.

"What about you, Tanya? You've deviated from your mission. At least I think you have."

"You're not my mission," she says, and she pinches my arm playfully.

She lies back and stares at the ceiling.

"I saw you and Howard together, I saw the way you cared about him. I've never seen that before. Then the three of us spent a lot of time together and we started to have fun, and it got in my mind somehow."

"So now we're both in trouble."

"In more ways than one," she says, and she slides her leg between mine, so we're twisted together like a pretzel.

"This is nice," I say.

"Yeah," she says with a sigh.

"Maybe too nice."

I feel her tense in my arms.

"What's that mean?" she says.

"I just mean it's inconvenient."

She pushes away from me, digging her knuckle into my bruised ribs as she goes. The pain flares.

"Inconvenient?" she says. "I'm sorry having sex with me doesn't fit comfortably into your briefing folder."

"Our lives are in danger, Tanya. And I have to find my father. It's not a good time to get distracted."

"To hell with you," she says, and she jumps out of bed, throwing on clothes as she goes.

"Wait a second!" I say, but she's not listening.

She rushes out the door and slams it behind her. I sit in bed for a minute, trying to figure out what went wrong.

Women.

There's not a lot of information about them in the training manual.

I WALK INTO THE KITCHEN.

Howard is eating a peanut butter and jelly sandwich.

"Howard, have you seen—"

"She just ran past me. She said she needed to take a walk. And she looked pissed."

I stand there, trying to figure out whether I should go after her.

He chews the sandwich, watching me.

"Are you in the doghouse?" he says.

"Where did you hear that expression?"

"That's what my dad used to say after he had a fight with my mom. *I'm in the doghouse big-time.*"

"Then I guess I'm in the doghouse," I say.

He nods like it's obvious.

"Are you hungry?" he says. "You haven't eaten in a while."

He offers me a peanut butter sandwich on a plate.

I'm thinking about next steps, what The Program's reaction might be to Father's death, and how I can keep us safe. But I have to have enough energy for what comes next.

"Definitely hungry," I say, and I take the sandwich he's given me, spread peanut butter on the top of it, and lay on another piece of bread to turn it into a triple-decker. When I'm finished constructing, I dig in.

"Wow. That's a lot of sandwich."

"I need energy to heal," I say.

"And to kick ass," Howard says. "I mean, if the need arises."

I smile. "That's right."

We eat in silence, but Howard keeps glancing up at me, then looking away.

"Just say it, Howard."

"I heard some noises upstairs before." He still won't look at me directly.

"What kinds of noises?"

"*Those* kinds of noises," he says. "I'm not stupid. I know what they mean."

"Things got a little complicated between me and Tanya."

"It's just—I don't know. It's kind of weird."

I can see he's uncomfortable. And I think I know why.

"Don't you have a girlfriend?" I say. "The one in Osaka. I saw you chatting with her on the computer in New York."

"That's Goji," he says. "She's my girlfriend online. But I've never had one in real life."

"And you thought Tanya was going to be your girlfriend."

"No!" he says, his face instantly turning red. "But she was really nice to me when we were locked in that room. And then we slept in the backseat together. I thought maybe she liked me. I guess it was just an act, huh?"

"She likes you for real. I know she does."

"She likes me as a friend. But she likes you a different way."

"Yeah."

"It figures," he says.

"Sometimes it happens like that. You like someone but they don't like you back. Or someone likes you that you don't like."

I'm thinking about Miranda on top of the building in Boston. I thought there was something special between us, but that didn't keep her from wanting to die. Or trying to kill me in the process.

"So you never know how it will go," I say. "I don't have a ton of experience with all this, but I think it's special when it happens for two people at the same time."

"So it's not a bad thing that she doesn't like me in that way?"

"Not if you don't make it a bad thing."

He nods, chewing on his sandwich.

"I'll do my best," he says. "Thanks for talking to me about this stuff, Zach."

I reach out and squeeze his shoulder.

"I don't think I've given anyone advice before," I say.

"You're good at it."

I finish off my sandwich and gulp down a glass of milk.

"Do you mind if I give you a little advice, too?" Howard says.

I shrug.

"You have to get out of the doghouse fast," he says. "If you stay there too long, it sort of becomes permanent. I think that's what happened to my folks. It started with one fight, then two, then they didn't talk to each other for fifteen years."

I think about how Howard was when I first met him, always home alone. I never did meet his parents or see them interact together. Now I know why.

"Good advice," I say.

I put down the empty glass and go outside to look for Tanya.

I PASS THROUGH THE GARAGE.

There's an old Jeep Wrangler there, keys hidden above the driver's visor where Tanya said they'd be.

I start the engine and find the tank full, just as Tanya said it would be, with no warning lights on the dash.

I turn off the car and leave the keys in the ignition.

I step out the side door of the garage to look for Tanya, but she's nowhere to be found.

I pause in the front yard and look around. We are in a rural area, no other houses in view. A plan is already forming in my mind. First, I need to recon the area, and then I have to ascertain my status with The Program.

I take three deep breaths to oxygenate my system, and I set out at a jog. I'm careful to make light contact with the pavement, attempting to keep my injured head from receiving too much vibration. Eventually my jog becomes a run. I use motion and blood flow to clean out my system and bring my senses back online. The peanut butter sandwich helps. The fresh air helps, too.

I scan the area in front and behind as I go, checking the main road that leads to the house, moving like someone out for his usual morning run. When I'm sure I'm not being watched, I dart into the woods that line one side of the street.

I run at a diagonal for about fifteen minutes until I pop out on a different road on an adjacent block. Then I do it again, cutting into the woods and running for five minutes. Twenty minutes of running at a moderate pace should put me three and a half miles from our location.

I stop at an area where the woods are most dense, and I turn on The Program phone. It instantly buzzes with a series of 911 text messages that I've missed. Messages from Mother trying to get in contact with me.

That means one of two things. She knows I'm alive and she's looking for me. Or she doesn't know whether I'm alive and she's trying to find out.

If there's a chance Mother thinks I'm dead and I call her, I'm putting myself back on the radar. But without speaking to her, I can't find out how much she knows and what her plan might be.

Every mission has turning points, moments of decision that will lead the proceedings in one direction or another.

I make such a decision now. I call Mother.

MOTHER SOUNDS WORRIED.

"You're alive." That's the first thing she says to me.

"Alive and well," I say.

"You look tired," she says.

That means Mother has remotely turned on my phone's camera. She's watching me, but I cannot see her. Knowing this, I do not change my facial expression at all. I will allow my face to reflect the feelings I want her to see, nothing more or less.

"I am tired. It's been a difficult few days," I say.

"We have a bird down," she says.

"I know."

"You were supposed to be on that helicopter, yet you're alive and others are not," Mother says.

"I imagine you have questions you want to ask me."

"I'm not going to ask. You can tell me what you want me to know."

It's possible Mother already knows what happened during the crash, and she wants me to incriminate myself. It's also possible that she doesn't know, and she's digging for information. I decide to stay as close to the truth as I can.

"I saw the helicopter go down," I say. "I watched it crash, but I couldn't do anything to stop it."

Technically true.

"We sent a team out there," Mother says. "Do you know what they found?"

"A mess."

"That's all you have to say?"

A moment later my screen flashes and Mother's image appears on the phone.

She's wearing a dark gray business suit and the same stylish glasses I saw before. Beneath them, her eyes are tight with rage.

"Let me explain how this looks from my side of the board," she says. "I get a call from Father telling me that you are walking toward the helicopter. My next call is from our tech-surveillance people informing me that a 911 operator is reporting smoke rising above a river in southern Pennsylvania. And this helicopter I sent—"

She hesitates for a moment, steadying herself before continuing.

"This helicopter I sent to pick you up and bring you home is a burning hulk on the ground. And the man—"

Her voice cracks.

"The man who was my partner of over ten years was on that helicopter. The man who built The Program with me, the one who educated you and treated you like his own son. That man disappeared in the burning wreckage of that helicopter. So you might imagine that I am upset, Zach. More upset than I have ever been, and I have been quite upset in my time."

She waits, watching me, her eyes intense even through the screen.

"I'm sorry," I say.

I show her sadness. It's not difficult to do. There is a part of me that is legitimately upset over what has happened.

"Are you sorry because you were involved, or are you sorry for my loss?"

Don't lie to her. Stay as close to the truth as possible.

"I'm sorry for both, Mother."

"So you were on the helicopter," she says.

"Yes."

"I see," she says. She adjusts her glasses. "It was you who brought down the helicopter."

"Not directly."

"Tell me what happened."

"Father gave the order for me to be drugged, and I reacted. There was a fight, one of the soldiers' guns went off, and the pilot was killed. It was unintentional."

"Why would he drug you?"

"He said he didn't trust me, and he wouldn't take me to you until he'd questioned me himself."

"That is highly unusual," Mother says.

"So you didn't order it?"

"I did not."

I sense an opening. This time I show her my anger, turning the energy of the conversation back on her.

"Let me tell you how things look from *my* side of the board, Mother. You send Father to pick me up, and he makes a move to capture me. I'm the one who has questions here. I'm the one who feels betrayed."

"Whatever your feelings, you let your Father die in that wreck."

"I tried to save him," I say. "It wasn't possible."

"Enough," Mother says. Her face turns to stone. "Your behavior is unforgivable."

"This is not what I wanted, Mother."

"What do you want?"

I want to find my father.

"I want to come home," I say. "But I need to know that what happened with Father won't happen again."

"Are you negotiating with me?"

"I'm asking for your protection."

Mother crosses her arms and shakes her head. "You think you still have options, but you're wrong. You don't have options anymore."

The sound of helicopter rotors in the distance, moving toward me.

The call has gone on longer than I intended. Mother has kept me talking long enough to divert resources in my direction.

"This was never a negotiation," Mother says.

The sound of the helicopter gets louder above me.

"I gave you a chance to come in on your own power, but you hurt us. Badly. Whatever Father did, your actions are unforgivable. So now we're coming for you, Zach. You've left us no choice."

Us.

Why would Mother change pronouns? Who is she referring to?

"Good-bye, Mother."

"For now," she says.

I power down the phone and slip it into my pocket.

I have no options. That's what Mother said.

But that's not what she's taught me. There are options, even in desperate circumstances. There are always options. To find them, I will need time.

So I run.

I USE EVERY INCH OF THE THREE MILES I'VE GIVEN MYSELF.

I run at breakneck speed through the wood line, across several neighborhoods, racing back to the house.

I burst through the side door, momentarily fearful of what I might find, but the fear dissipates, unable to take hold with the neuro-suppressor inside me.

I race through the kitchen and into the living room. Howard is reading an old novel from the bookcase.

"We have to go!" I shout.

He jumps out of his chair and the book drops to the floor, the cover splayed open. It's a Hemingway novel, *A Farewell to Arms*.

I say, "Grab your things and get to the garage. We're leaving in two minutes."

"Tanya's back," he says. "She's upstairs."

"Two minutes!" I say.

Tanya's not in the bathroom or the first bedroom. I open the door of the second bedroom, startling Tanya in the process.

She's in her underwear, pulling on a pair of jeans. She is gorgeous, her skin tanned golden brown, her breasts pressed into a familiar blue-and-white sports bra.

She looks at me with a strange expression on her face. She's holding a cell phone I haven't seen before.

"Whose phone is that?"

"Mine," she says.

"A Program phone?"

"Yes."

"You didn't have it when I searched you."

"I hid it behind the seat before I got out of the car."

"So you had it all this time?"

"I had it, but I didn't use it until now. Mother just called."

I hear a door open and close downstairs. Howard going out to the garage.

"Mother knows we're together, Zach. She gave me orders to bring you in."

"And if I won't go?"

She doesn't answer.

She doesn't have to. We both know the answer.

"So what are you going to do?" I ask.

I steady myself, preparing for what will come next. Tanya and I, fighting until one of us cannot fight anymore.

"I'm going to ignore the orders," Tanya says, as if it's obvious.

"Why?"

"I just got a boyfriend. I'm not going to give him up."

I smile.

"Boyfriend? This is moving a little fast, don't you think?"

She puts her hands on her hips. "On second thought, maybe I will turn you in."

"We have to get moving," I say.

"Agreed."

I start to go, but I pause at the door.

Get out of the doghouse fast. That's what Howard told me.

"About earlier. I said some stupid things."

"No kidding," she says. "You were a real asshole."

"I was going to use a different word, but yeah, you're right. I'm not used to, you know—"

"Relationships?"

"I'm not very good at them."

"You're better than you think," she says with a smile. "Apology accepted. Now how about we get the hell out of here?"

"You want to put on a shirt before we go?"

"I don't know, I thought I might wear a bra for this part of the mission."

"That's okay with me," I say.

"You're such a guy," she says.

She pulls on her shirt. "What are you thinking in terms of a plan?"

"Short term, we drop off the grid."

"Head northeast," she says. "Maybe into Canada."

"Good idea," I say. "There might be camping gear in the house. If not, we'll buy some on the road."

"I saw a storage shed in the backyard."

"I'll go and check. Grab whatever else you can find, and I'll meet you in the garage."

"One more thing before you go," she says.

She rushes forward and kisses me.

"What was that for?" I say.

"Do I need a reason?"

HOWARD ISN'T IN THE GARAGE.

The back of the Jeep is open and half-filled with food and supplies. I call Howard's name inside the house, but I don't get an answer.

I have to find him. Now.

I quickly check the perimeter of the house, ending up in the backyard near the storage shed.

"Nice to see you again, Zach."

It's Mike. He steps out of the shadows by the side of the house. He has Howard next to him, clamped by the elbow. Howard's face is pale.

"Don't hurt him," I say. "He's innocent."

"He *was* innocent, but not anymore. You signed his death warrant the moment you told him who you were. That was back in New York, wasn't it?"

"Yes," I say. No need to lie now. It's more important to keep Mike engaged and talking. Lying to him is only going to make him angry.

"That girl in New York, she's the one who turned you."

"She didn't turn me," I say.

Samara's face appears to me, dark curls falling to her shoulders the way she looked the first time I saw her.

"It had nothing to do with her," I say. "I had faulty orders, and I tried to set things right."

"There are no faulty orders. Only faulty soldiers."

"You helped me in New York," I say. "You knew I deviated, and you kept my secret. Whose orders were you following?"

"It wasn't about orders. I kept your secret because I wanted you alive. I thought you were redeemable."

"I'm more than redeemable. I'm an asset," I say.

"An asset to who?"

Howard struggles to get free, and Mike clamps down harder on his shoulder.

"Let him go, Mike."

"That's not going to happen. I don't really give two shits about this kid, but you do. And I'd like to know why."

"He's my friend."

"There are no friends. Not for people like us."

"People like you, Mike. Not me."

"Oh man, now I'm really feeling bad about myself."

"Maybe you can go to therapy and talk about it."

Mike's gaze shifts behind me, and he smiles.

"Looks like it's going to be group therapy," he says.

Tanya appears behind me. I feel something sharp and metallic against the back of my neck.

"There is a knife against your spine," she says loudly. "If you move, I will paralyze you."

I can't see her face, but her voice is steel, no trace of the Tanya who kissed me a moment ago.

Mike says, "Program ahead, Program behind. What's a traitor to do?"

I can feel the pressure high on my neck, the blade touching flesh between my C1 and C2 vertebrae.

Mike gestures to Tanya. "Bring him to me. Slowly."

She hesitates. "I have capture orders," she says.

"I'm overriding them," Mike says.

"They come directly from Mother."

"I'm the commander in the field," Mike says. "Right now, my authority trumps hers."

"What are you planning to do with him?"

"Not your concern," he says. "I take full responsibility. Now bring him to me."

"Yes, sir," she says.

Tanya nudges me forward, and I resist.

"Don't fight me," she says.

She gets me moving with a knee to the back of my thigh.

As the shock of Tanya's betrayal fades, I focus on a way to disarm her. Mike must sense this, because his grip on Howard becomes a stranglehold.

Howard chokes and looks at me, his eyes desperate.

I take slow steps, allowing Tanya and her knife to set the agenda.

"This is beautiful," Mike says. "I should have known it would take a cute girl with a knife to bring you down. You love girls and you hate knives. It's the perfect combination."

"I'm glad you're enjoying yourself," I say.

"You don't get it, do you? I tried everything to save you and bring you back to The Program. It's your fault we're here now."

Howard grimaces from the pressure Mike is putting on his neck.

"You wandered, you deviated, you questioned," Mike says. "Everything you've been trained *not* to do, you did. I thought it was growing pains, but no more."

"What do you think now?"

"I think you're broken, and broken things need to be discarded."

I continue to move toward Mike, prompted by Tanya's knife.

"You're going to let him kill me?" I ask Tanya.

Tanya whispers in my ear. "Trust," she says.

Mike knocks Howard to the ground.

Tanya directs me forward, delivering me into Mike's hands, her knife still at my neck. I'm within striking distance of Mike, but I do not make a move.

Trust.

Mike reaches for me. "Good job," he says to Tanya.

That's when she strikes.

She uses my body as cover to camouflage a knife attack against Mike. I feel the blade withdraw from my neck, then Tanya pushes me away as she simultaneously leaps forward, planting the knife deep in Mike's side.

He howls in rage and jumps back, grasping the handle of the knife that is inside him, using his flesh like a sheath to prevent Tanya from withdrawing the weapon and striking at him a second time.

With his free hand, he pulls a gun from his pocket.

Tanya freezes in place.

I watch Mike's gun barrel track from one of us to the next. Three shots, three kills. He's more than capable of it.

I assess the knife in Mike's side, measuring the blood seeping through the fabric of his shirt. It is a survivable wound, high on his right quadrant. It may have punctured his lung, but nothing more.

The wound has to hurt, but that will not stop someone like Mike.

I know because it wouldn't stop me.

Mike stares at Tanya, his eyes glassy with pain. "What did Zach do to you?"

"He didn't do anything," she says. "It was me. I made a choice."

"To leave The Program?"

"Not exactly. It's more like I chose him over you."

He looks from me to Tanya and back. Howard pulls himself up from the ground and stands by us.

Mike says, "Bad things happen to the people who care about Zach. Friends, girlfriends. They have a habit of dying. But I'm sure he told you that, didn't he?"

I glance at Tanya, a plan communicated silently between us. I indicate for her to move left as I move right toward Howard. The more distance between us, the longer it will take for Mike to adjust and complete his shots, and the higher the survival percentage in this scenario.

Mike says, "Come to think of it, there's not a friend of yours who has survived a mission, is there, Zach? Except the mayor of New York. And he's been in mourning since he met you."

The mayor trusted me enough to let me into his home, and he gave me his blessing to date his daughter. Now she's dead, and his life is changed forever. Mike knows the story, and he's rubbing my face in it.

He wants me to suffer before I die. I will not give him the satisfaction.

Mike brings up the pistol, preparing to fire.

I jump away from Tanya, knowing that even though I will be shot, the added distance between us will increase her odds of survival as Mike resets for a second shot.

I brace myself as I fall—

But the gun does not go off.

When I look back, Mike has disappeared.

I glance over at Tanya. She's as confused as I am.

"Where did he go?" I say.

"He disappeared through the bushes," she says.

"Why?"

"I have no idea," she says.

Tanya grabs Howard, checking him for injury.

"I'm okay," he says. "Just scared."

I run to the place where Mike was standing. There's no trace of him.

"Maybe he was hurt worse than we thought?" I say.

"No, he could have fought with that wound," she says. "It's my fault. I went for a kill strike, but he moved at the last second and I missed the mark."

"You still saved our lives," I say. "I figured either you turned, or you'd been lying to us all along."

"Did I scare you?" she asks.

"Not a chance," I say.

"You scared the crap out of me," Howard says.

"Thank you," she says, pleased with herself.

"What's the plan?" Howard asks.

I imagine Mike's next move will be reporting back to The Program, maybe blowing the whistle on Tanya. If so, The Program will be after us with a vengeance.

"I'm thinking we stick with the plan," I say. "What about you, Tanya?"

"I agree," Tanya says. "Let's get off the grid fast."

I kick open the storage shed, hoping to find camping supplies or outdoor survival gear. But there's nothing we can use.

"What now?" Tanya says.

"It's time to go shopping," I say.

THE ELECTRIC DOORS OF A KMART SLIDE OPEN.

I'm hit by a wave of ice-cold department store air. Howard takes a deep breath.

"Feels nice," he says.

"Don't get comfortable," I say. "We're in and out of here as fast as possible."

I scan the floor. It's a big Kmart, so it should have a decent selection of outdoor equipment, especially in this part of the state, which is filled with parks and hiking trails.

"I'll hit the camping section," I say to Tanya.

"Great. I'll see what I can find in the self-defense arena. Howard, you want to come with me or stay with Zach?"

She turns, but Howard is already disappearing down an aisle.

"I'll get him," I say.

She nods and moves quickly into the depths of the store.

I look around, concerned for a moment, until I notice the sign for ELECTRONICS. If I know Howard...

Sure enough, I find him standing in the television section, his attention focused on a wall of screens.

"Hey, buddy, we have to get going," I say.

"Why are you on TV?" he says.

I look at the TV monitors. My face is splashed across every screen, the words TEEN TERRORIST beneath it.

The volume is muted, so I read the closed captioning running across the set:

DANIEL MARTIN, 16, SUSPECTED IN THE BOMBING OF THE FEDERAL BUILDING IN BOSTON...

Daniel Martin. That was my cover name on the last mission against Eugene Moore and his military-training camp.

It's The Program. They've leaked my picture to the press, accusing me of being one of the Boston bombers. For some reason they've gone public, burning my identity and making me the most sought-after fugitive in the country in the process.

I pull the baseball cap lower over my eyes.

"Let's get away from these screens," I say to Howard.

This time he listens, following me as I move back toward the housewares section.

"Why are they saying those things about you?" Howard asks.

"I'm wondering the same thing. Tanya said The Program had put a capture order on me, so why go public and bring the authorities into it?"

"Maybe they're trying to smoke you out?" Howard says.

"It doesn't make sense," I say. "If my identity is public, they lose the ability to take me in secret, and they risk my getting shot or killed during capture."

Unless they've written me off completely, and they don't care.

I imagine Mike calling Mother, telling her that Tanya has turned because I corrupted her. Mother decides that I am a danger to The Program, a danger so great that they need me dead by any means.

But why would Mike do that when he could have killed me himself and taken the credit? He would choose the path that benefits him the most. How would it help him for The Program to go public with my information?

Tanya rushes through the store to find us.

"You need to look outside right now," she says.

We follow her until we can see out the front windows.

Police cars are pouring into the shopping center entrance. I note a large SWAT tactical truck already in place at the side of the Kmart. The back doors of the truck are flung open, and a dozen SWAT officers start fanning out around the perimeter of the store.

"Are they here for us?" Tanya asks.

"For me," I say.

"We were in the TV section," Howard says. "Zach is on the news."

Tanya looks at me.

"The Program burned you?"

"They're saying I was involved in the bombing at the JFK building."

"Were you?" Tanya asks.

"I was there," I say.

I don't need to tell her I was on a mission to stop the bombing. She can guess as much.

"So there's a SWAT team about to storm Kmart," Tanya says.

"I always thought shopping was boring," Howard says.

"Not today," I say.

Uniformed cops are rushing scared Kmart shoppers to the edges of the parking lot, where they crouch behind a line of squad cars parked hood to bumper. That means the SWAT team is going to storm the building, rather than playing it safe and waiting for the feds.

"They're only after me," I say. "So I want you two to get out of here. Walk out like you're scared shoppers, and let the police lead you away to safety. I don't think The Program is here yet, which means you should have a head start."

"I'm not leaving without you," Tanya says.

"Get Howard to safety," I say.

"Like hell," Howard says. "I'm not leaving, either."

"Listen, guys, I appreciate the sentiment, but it's not the time to play hero. I can't keep you safe if you stay here."

"You don't have to keep me safe," Tanya says. "I keep myself safe."

"Me, too," Howard says, though it's a lot less convincing coming from him.

"So what's the plan? You're going to form a human shield?" I say.

"Whatever you need," Tanya says.

He and Tanya stand together, arms crossed.

"If you're serious, then we'd better get to work," I say.

"I'll see what I can find to help us," Tanya says, and she disappears down an aisle.

"What about me?" Howard says. "Where do you want me?"

"I want you as far away from the action as possible. You can't be fighting trained SWAT officers. They'll be carrying weapons and wearing full body armor."

I'm looking for a place to put Howard during the assault. A back room or storage area. That's when I notice a ladder in the hardware section.

"Up," I say to Howard.

"What's up?"

"That's where I'm going to put you."

I hear a whistle behind me. I turn to see Tanya standing down the end of the aisle, her arms cradling a box of road flares.

A plan begins to come together.

THE SMOKE DRIFTS IN WAVES, MOVING ACROSS THE STORE ON AIR-CONDITIONED CURRENTS.

Tanya and I jog together from aisle to aisle, lighting flares and dropping them as we go.

Howard is hidden high in the luggage section breathing through a painter's respirator mask. He should be okay up there for at least ten minutes. If we haven't made it out of the store by then, we will be dead or in custody, and Howard can climb down and pretend he was an innocent bystander caught in the assault.

I pop the last of the flares and fling it across the floor. Tanya steps out of the smoke in front of me. She's carrying a camping ax, a short black handle fronted with a sharp silver blade. She spins it in her hand.

"Don't be jealous. I've got one for you, too," she says.

"No bladed weapons," I say. "I don't want to hurt anyone if we don't have to."

"They'll have shoot-to-kill orders, Zach."

"They're regular cops who are following orders, and they believe they're confronting a terrorist. No lethal weapons unless and until we're out of options."

"No *lethal* weapons," she says, "But that doesn't mean no weapons at all."

"No, it doesn't."

"Back in a flash," she says, and she disappears into the smoke.

She's back twenty seconds later with a set of titanium baseball bats.

"How about these to get us started?" she says.

"Perfect," I say.

I hear glass shattering in the back of the store.

"They're coming," I say.

"Let's split up. I'll take out as many as I can, then I'll make my way back here—"

She peers through the smoke, trying to find a sign to locate our position.

"Housewares," I say.

"Great," she says. "We can fight these guys, then pick out curtains for our new place."

"You are really starting to worry me," I say, and she laughs.

I hear the telltale roar of a flash-bang grenade from the back of the store, the effect like lightning through the smoke.

Tanya expertly spins a bat and flips it under her arm.

"Showtime," she says.

DARK FIGURES MOVE THROUGH THE SMOKE.

A dozen SWAT team members enter through the back of the store clad in black body armor carrying HK MP5 submachine guns. They follow standard tactical procedure as they enter, threading in from a single point, then splitting into two groups to fan out around the perimeter.

It would be an effective strategy in most situations.

Not this one.

The danger of standardized strategy is just that—it's standardized. I'm very familiar with their training protocol, so I know what they're going to do before they do it.

Twelve team members, split six and six. Half for me, half for Tanya.

I use the smoke as cover, and I pick them off one by one, starting at the end of the line and working my way forward. I use the baseball bat to accomplish a choke grip at the neckline, the weakest point in their body armor.

I take out three of them before the next officer senses that something is wrong. As I approach, he whirls around and sees me coming at him through the smoke. He brings up the MP5 to fire, and I leap the last five feet, swinging the bat at the barrel of the weapon as he fires, the burst going high and shattering a row of lights across the ceiling above us.

I track the direction of the rounds, concerned that they're headed toward the luggage section, where Howard is hidden. When they hear the shots, SWAT guys one and two break position and scatter.

That leaves me face-to-face with number three. He grunts and strikes out, using the butt of the machine gun to attack. I counter with the bat, sparks flying as titanium strikes metal once, twice, then the SWAT member falls back, frustrated, dropping his grip from the machine gun and reaching for a sidearm.

I drop the bat, jumping at him as he struggles to bring up his pistol. I grab his helmet and twist hard, the torque on his neck pulling his body down and off center where my knee is coming up to meet him. One strike to the belly to disorient him, a second to take him down, and a third to the head to knock him out.

The smoke is dispersing at ground level now, most of it rising to the ceiling, where it is useless as cover.

Rounds explode into the floor at my feet. I see the flash of a muzzle firing at me from ten feet away. I leap and scurry up a row of shelves into the smoke cloud. I stay high, crabbing across the shelves until I drop down on the officer from above, surprising him and quickly knocking him unconscious.

"*Stop!*" a voice shouts.

Another SWAT officer has seen me. He points his weapon at me from a few feet away, his aim true through the thinning smoke.

I raise my arms above my head and slowly rise to standing, my eyes flitting from place to place, looking for a way out.

"Don't move," he says.

He advances toward me cautiously. Six feet away, then four, his free hand reaching for the zip ties on his belt. If he cuffs me, it's game over.

Just then, Tanya appears out of the smoke, snatching him from behind and quickly taking him down with an elbow to the throat. She pulls the zip ties from his belt, rolls him, then handcuffs him behind his back.

Smart. I should have been doing that all along myself.

I hear footsteps behind and turn to find a group of SWAT officers on top of us. They've realized they're targeting professionals and they've wised up, massing their remaining forces for an attack. They rush in, dividing Tanya and me, attempting to overwhelm us with sheer numbers.

I aim a low kick to the first man's knee, and I feel the sickening snap as it gives way, knocking him down.

Before I can reset myself, another officer grabs me from behind and pulls me back toward him, exposing my belly to the air.

I see Tanya in the aisle across from me, taking down a guy with an expert triple kick that moves from stomach, to neck, to head.

I fight the man behind me, flinging my head back to try and smash into his nose, but he dodges and tightens his grip. I can feel ropy muscle in his arms holding me tight against him.

Suddenly Tanya rushes toward us, planting herself at the last moment, and directing a vicious kick at my crotch.

I wince in expectation of the blow, but she pushes the kick forward at the last second, clearing my groin and instead kicking the balls of the guy behind me.

He lets go with a terrible moan as the wind is forced from his lungs. He sags against my back, and I spin and take him down, finishing the job.

The fire alarm goes off, and a moment later the sprinklers release, water pouring down on us from above.

I turn back to Tanya.

"Do you know how close that kick was?" I say.

"About this close?" she says, making a small finger gesture.

I frown.

"Hey, it's not personal," she says. "I got the job done."

I take a moment to orient myself. Tanya and I are standing in housewares, SWAT guys splayed on the floor all around us, water raining down from the ceiling and pooling at our feet.

"I guess everything went according to plan," I say.

"Are you kidding?" Tanya says. "The curtains are ruined."

I laugh. "Let's find Howard and get going," I say.

"I'm right here!" Howard says. He comes jogging around the corner wearing a catcher's mask and carrying a baseball bat in either hand.

"I told you to stay in hiding," I say.

"One of them got too close," he says.

I can see dents in the metal of the bats.

"Did you fight a SWAT officer?" I say.

"I guess I did," he says in disbelief.

"Damn. Howard's a badass," Tanya says.

Howard smiles.

"We'll celebrate later," I say. "We've got about a hundred cops out for blood in the parking lot."

"How are we going to get past them?" Howard says.

"Uniforms," I say, pointing at the fallen officers. "Put them on."

We quickly strip three of the SWAT members, slipping their uniforms on over our clothes. I search the remaining officers until I find the lead and pull a set of keys and a cell phone from his belt.

When I get back, I look at Tanya and Howard dressed as SWAT team members. They are believable if you don't look too closely.

"Now we're going out the way they came in," I say.

"How can we do that?" Howard says.

"Swagger," I say.

And we walk straight out the back door.

The minute we hit pavement, a police lieutenant comes running up to me. "What's going on in there?" he shouts. "We lost contact."

I cough and double over, wincing like I've been hurt.

"We need more men," I say.

"And women," Tanya says.

"I'm heading back to the truck to call it in," I say.

"Shit, I knew we should have waited," the lieutenant says, and he rushes off.

I keep walking and Tanya and Howard follow me. I see the SWAT truck parked around the side of the building and we head for it.

"We're stealing their truck?" Howard says.

"They don't need it," Tanya says. "They're going to be at the hospital for a while."

I take out the keys I snagged from the lead officer. One slips easily into the lock on the back of the truck, and the doors swing open. Howard climbs in, eyeing the combat gear and equipment.

"Awesome," he says.

I jog to the front and unlock the driver's door. Tanya hoists herself inside.

"Do you want me to drive?" she says.

"My turn," I say.

She nods and climbs into the passenger seat. I light up the engine and feel it roar beneath us.

"Have you ever driven one of these?" Tanya asks.

"I can build one of these," I say.

I throw it into gear and drive slowly past about a dozen squad cars. I salute a couple of officers who are staring at us, perhaps surprised to see SWAT retreating. They return the salute, then focus back toward Kmart, not realizing the people they are looking for are making an escape right in front of them.

COPS ARE DESCENDING ON THE AREA FROM EVERY DIRECTION.

Tanya says, "Once they discover that we escaped, everyone in the world will be looking for us."

"We can't outrun the whole world," Howard adds.

"I don't think Canada's an option anymore," Tanya says.

"I agree," I say.

"Do we have any options?" Howard asks.

There's silence in the SWAT truck as each of us considers the answer.

The Program has played the ultimate trump card, destroying my anonymity and risking its own in order to guarantee that I'll be apprehended.

How can I defeat the biggest bully on the block?

"It's David versus Goliath," Howard says. Then he sighs deeply. "I wish it were Goliath versus Goliath."

"That's brilliant," I say.

"What's brilliant?" Howard says.

"You just gave me an idea."

I reach for my phone. There's a secret file that I've carried with me, a photo of a certain business card I was given—it feels like a long time ago now.

We're far enough away from the Kmart that I can risk pulling over for a moment.

"I'm going to hop out and make a call," I say.

"Who are you calling?" Tanya asks.

"Goliath," I say.

IT RINGS FOUR TIMES.

A familiar voice picks up.

"Yes?"

That's all he says.

"It's me," I say.

I can sense the hesitation on the other end of the line.

"Benjamin?" the voice asks. It's the name he knows me by, the name I was using when we first met.

There's practically nothing I can say over the phone. I tell him only that I need his help and that he might be the only one in the world who can help me.

It wouldn't surprise me if he hung up and we never spoke to each other again. He has every reason to turn me down. I'm asking him to put his entire career—maybe even his life—on the line.

But he doesn't turn me down. He says two words.

"Saratoga Springs."

It's an invitation.

I ditched the SWAT truck back in Pennsylvania, trading it for a black Mustang with a 5.0L V8 engine. We rumble past the historic mansions of Saratoga Springs, an affluent city where racing money comes to play.

There's a baseball field near our destination with a game in progress. Teenagers take the field while their parents watch from folding chairs set up along the sidelines. As we pull up, a guy hits a hard double into left field, and the crowd rises in a crescendo of cheers.

"We drove all this way for a baseball game?" Tanya asks. "You must really love sports, huh?"

"Seriously, what are we doing here? Tell us the secret," Howard says.

I stop the Mustang and watch the baseball player round second, start for third, then decide not to risk it and back up.

I played in a baseball game like this not too long ago.

A different mission. A different life.

I've lived many lives in the last two years. I'm supposed to forget each one after it happens—absorb the lessons, then move on, blending into the next life, the next mission, forever moving forward and always remaining anonymous.

I've been trained to forget, but that became impossible to do after I met Samara and her father, the mayor of New York City.

Howard said our battle was David versus Goliath, and he wished it were Goliath versus Goliath. This is where Goliath can be found.

His summer home is down the street from this baseball field, an enormous mansion set back from the road and surrounded by a tall stone wall.

I find a parking spot by the field, down at the end of a long line of cars. Then I explain to Tanya and Howard why we've come to this place, and why I'm leaving them at the baseball game while I go to the mayor's house.

"I should come with you," Howard says. "The mayor knows me."

He's right about that. Once upon a time, the mayor's daughter, Samara, had befriended Howard. For a while, she was his only friend. But Samara is gone now, and I'm not sure how the mayor is going to react when he finds out why I'm here.

"I have to do this alone," I tell Howard. "But if everything goes as planned, I'll need you both to back up my story. One of the mayor's people will come out to get you. You'll know I've sent him, because he won't use your real names."

"What will he call us?"

"How about Bonnie and Clyde?" I say.

"Awesome," Howard says.

Tanya attempts a smile.

"What if it's not one of the mayor's people," Tanya says. "What if the police come? What if we're caught?"

"It's up to you how much you want to reveal, Tanya. But, Howard, I want you to tell them your story."

"How much of my story?" Howard says.

"All of it. If they come, you tell all. Don't leave anything out."

"New York?" Howard says, his voice low.

"What happened in New York?" Tanya says.

"Tell them what you know," I say to Howard, ignoring Tanya for the time being. "Don't speculate. Stick to the facts, and you'll be fine."

"What happened in New York?" Tanya says again.

Howard looks at me, unsure how much he should reveal.

"We lost a friend," I say.

Tanya looks at me curiously.

"The less you know, the easier it will be for you," I say. "If I answer your questions, you might have to talk about it later."

"I'm not crazy about this plan," Tanya says.

"Do you have a better one?"

She bites at her lower lip. "I have a different one. Not better."

"Will you trust me on this?"

"I already trust you," she says. "Why stop now?"

"Okay, then," I say, and I pass her the car keys. From the scoreboard on the field, I can see the game won't be over for a couple of hours. "If you haven't heard from me by the time the game is over, leave with the crowd. Don't stick around."

They nod gravely. I get out of the car.

"Wait, Zach."

It's Tanya. She's slipped out of the backseat and she's coming toward me.

I stop. Tanya stands in front of me, our breath in sync.

"How many times have we said good-bye in the last forty-eight hours?" Tanya asks.

"Too many."

"Let's make this the last time."

She kisses me, softly at first, and then the kiss turns urgent, the two of us clinging to each other.

A cheer goes up from the crowd behind us as a player makes a hit.

I let Tanya go.

"See you soon," I say.

And I turn and head for the mayor's house.

I NOTE THE SECURITY CAMERAS SUSPENDED ABOVE THE GATE.

In ten seconds I will be in range of their lenses. Everything I do from that moment on will be recorded.

I do not hesitate. I walk right up to the gate, where a black call box is embedded in a stone column.

I press the call button. It takes less than a minute for a gruff voice to come on the line.

"Speak."

"The mayor is expecting me," I say.

A moment later the gate buzzes open.

It's a long walk down a driveway that's practically its own road. A sprawling nineteenth-century estate house comes into view. There's a big man in a dark, well-tailored suit waiting for me. I recognize him as one of the mayor's longtime security detail, a man I last saw at Gracie Mansion. I call him the Pro.

"I'm going to pat you down," he says.

"Just like old times," I say.

"Yeah, I'm feeling very sentimental right now."

"I thought that was a tear in your eye."

"Arms up and spread your legs," he says.

He steps forward to search me.

"If we're going to have a problem, tell me now," he says.

"Is witty banter a problem?"

"If I was in your shoes, I wouldn't be in such a good mood."

"I'm in a terrible mood. Joking makes it a little easier."

He nods. "I feel you on that one, brother."

He searches me, professional but not overly aggressive. At least until he feels the weight in my jacket pocket. He grasps the back of my neck with one hand while he reaches in and pulls out two cell phones, both powered off. One is my Program phone, the other I took off the SWAT commander.

"Two phones?" he says.

"My mom's a worrier."

He nods, a half smile on his lips.

"Okay, superstar. Let's bring you to the boss."

He pauses at the door.

"Our past relationship notwithstanding, if you make any kind of move that concerns me, I will take you down. No questions asked."

"I appreciate the warning."

"One per customer," he says. "That's all you get."

He gestures for me to walk through the door in front of him.

I open a massive set of double doors and step into a grand foyer that smells of antique wood and history.

"Nice place," I say.

"Do me a favor—don't burn it down like you did the last one."

A moment later I hear footsteps approaching the foyer, and Mayor Goldberg appears. The Pro tenses next to me, ready for anything.

The mayor looks tired, and he seems to have aged in the short time since we last saw each other.

"Benjamin?" he says.

"It's me, sir."

"They're calling you Daniel Martin on the news."

"That's not my real name. Neither is Benjamin."

"I thought that might be the case," he says.

"Thank you for taking my call, sir. And for agreeing to meet with me."

"Aiding and abetting a suspected terrorist. I think they call that political suicide. But you risked your life for me at Gracie Mansion. More importantly, you risked your life for Samara."

Technically true. I risked my life to save her, then I risked my mission to try to redeem her. When neither of those succeeded, I did my job and I killed her.

The mayor doesn't know this, and he never will.

"I agreed to meet with you because I owe you one," the mayor says. "And I always repay my debts."

"I appreciate that," I say.

"Welcome to my home," he says. "Now come in and tell me why your face is on every television screen in the world."

THE MAYOR TAKES ME INTO THE DEN.

He immediately goes to a wet bar on the side of the room, pours himself two fingers of whiskey. He's obviously nervous, but covering it well.

"Diet Coke okay for you?" he says.

"I'll take a regular Coke if you have it."

The Pro lingers in the background, watching me intently.

The mayor passes me a glass, then takes a seat on the sofa across from me.

"You said your name is not Benjamin or Daniel. What should I call you?"

"Zach. That's my real name."

The mayor sips from his glass.

"The press is saying you were involved in the Boston bombings."

"I knew Lee Moore. He was a friend of mine."

His father, Eugene Moore, ran a training camp for teen terrorists. When I killed Moore, his son took over. That was the one thing I didn't expect.

"So you *were* involved?" the mayor says, his back stiffening.

"I was in the building when the bomb went off. I was trying to prevent it."

"The size of that explosion—if you were in the building, you wouldn't be alive, would you?"

"I was on the roof. I got out in time."

"You flew away?"

"In a manner of speaking. I was picked up by a helicopter."

"I don't remember seeing a rescue like that on the news."

"It wasn't on the news. Just like Gracie wasn't on the news. A lot of things happen and never make the news."

"Point taken," the mayor says. "But if you were there, you must have known what was going to happen."

The mayor is as clever as I remember, asking me questions with the precision of a prosecuting attorney.

"I suspected it would happen," I say. "That's not the same as knowing."

"So you were an innocent bystander who decided to try to stop a terrorist attack."

"No, sir. I was on assignment."

"What kind of assignment?" the mayor asks.

I glance at the Pro.

"I know you want your security man here," I say, "but what I'm about to tell you will put you both in danger."

The Pro steps forward. "More danger than we're already in by letting a suspected terrorist into the house?" he asks.

"Much more," I say.

He and the mayor share a look.

"Do you want to leave?" the mayor asks him.

The Pro shakes his head.

The mayor nods. "Then let's continue," he says to me.

"You asked about my assignment," I say. "I'm a soldier. My mission was to infiltrate Eugene Moore's training camp and disrupt his operation. The bombing was an outgrowth of that mission."

"A soldier?" the mayor says. He leans forward, taps down his glasses with two fingers and looks at me over the frames. "How old are you?"

"Sixteen."

"If you're sixteen, you're still in school."

"I finished school. I completed my studies on an accelerated timeline," I say.

"So you're in college now. Maybe ROTC?"

I shake my head.

"I was on assignment in Boston. Before that I was in New York, where we met."

"On assignment?" the mayor asks.

"Yes."

"You had something to do with the fire at Gracie Mansion."

"You and I both know it wasn't a fire," I say.

"You were there and you saw the shooting. So, of course, you know it was some kind of an attack."

"It wasn't just any attack. It was a plot by a rogue element of the Mossad posing as Arab terrorists. They planted explosives in the electrics room under Gracie, then they fanned out through the mansion disguised as members of the Israeli security detail."

"That's classified information," the mayor says.

"I have security clearance," I say.

"So you work for a security consultancy? You're an intelligence analyst, a young computer expert with access to the database?"

"Like I said, I'm a soldier."

"There are many kinds of soldiers."

"My skills are highly specialized. I'm trained as an assassin."

"Oh, you're an assassin," the Pro says. "That explains everything."

"I'm telling you the truth," I say.

"You're like a ninja?" the Pro asks.

"This isn't a joke."

"Ninjas are no joke," he says. "They come at night, dressed in black, totally invisible. I don't want to mess with ninjas."

The mayor holds up his hand to silence him.

"Zach, can you see why we might have trouble believing the things you're telling us?"

"Of course. But look at the facts. You know I was at Gracie, and the media have confirmed that I was in Boston. That's two major terror incidents in the course of one month. That would be quite a coincidence for a normal sixteen-year-old boy."

"Agreed," the mayor says.

"Before New York, I was in Natick, Massachusetts. Did you know Chen Wu, CEO of DefenseTech? He died last month."

"I didn't know him personally, but I heard the story."

"There were missions before that. Many of them. I can give you details if you need further confirmation."

"Let's assume you're telling us the truth," the mayor says. "Why did you call me?"

I stand, look from one man to the other. It's now or never.

"I'm in trouble," I say.

"No kidding," the Pro says.

"It's not what it looks like in the media. I'm being set up by the organization I work for. If it was just me in danger, I would deal with it alone. But there are other people involved. Innocent people."

I look at the mayor, wondering if I can trust him. But I've come too far to go back now.

"My father's life is in danger," I say. "He's a prisoner, and he's being held by my employers."

"*Your employers.* Who is it you work for?" the mayor asks.

"The government."

"I work for the government, too."

"It's a different government, Mr. Mayor. A shadow organization called The Program."

The mayor puts his drink down on the table. I notice the Pro shuffling slightly from leg to leg.

"That's a rather ominous name," the mayor says. "It's a Homeland Security operation?"

"Not directly."

"It sounds like you don't know who the hell you work for," the Pro says.

"I know who I report to. But you're correct, I don't know exactly who I work for, not in the broader sense."

"You just follow orders, huh?" the Pro says glibly.

"Don't you?" I ask.

The smirk disappears from his face.

"Why don't we call your boss and confirm all this?" the Pro says.

He takes out the cell phones he removed from my pocket earlier.

"I wouldn't turn that on," I say.

"There are two of them," the Pro says.

"The Samsung belongs to a very pissed-off SWAT commander. The iPhone is something else entirely. I'd suggest you don't touch it at all."

He holds up the iPhone, examining it in the light.

"It looks like a normal iPhone to me," he tells the mayor.

"There's a secure operating system hidden beneath the surface. It links to The Program."

"So if I turn this phone on—" the Pro says.

"They come for us. More precisely, for me. But they might be willing to take both of you out if it assures their getting to me."

The Pro says, "You're sitting next to one of the most powerful men in the world. You're saying this Program of yours would risk killing him?"

"Not directly. They might raid the building and we would all die in the process, a hostage crisis that went bad. They might blow up the house and call it a terrorist bombing, blame it on me. Do you want me to continue?"

The Pro says, "You have a great imagination, kid."

"It would be a mistake to think I'm making this up," I say.

"Tell me about your father," the mayor says.

He's asking questions. That's a good sign.

"I haven't seen my father in almost five years," I say. "I thought he was dead until a couple of weeks ago. Now I believe differently."

"He's been a prisoner for five years?" the mayor says.

"He's a scientist," I say. "They're forcing him to work for The Program. And I'm their bargaining chip."

The mayor sighs. "This is quite a story, Zach."

"I know it is. It's a lot to process all at once. But I'm not just asking you to believe in the story."

"What are you asking?"

"Believe in me," I say.

The mayor studies me for a moment. "I believe you enough to let you into my house."

I exhale, the tension lifting from my chest.

"What do you want me to do?" the mayor says. "How can I help you and your father?"

"Get on the phone. Call government officials you know, call your friends in law enforcement, say whatever you have to say to get them to the house. The more powerful people who know my story, the safer we are."

"And if I have doubts about you?" the mayor asks.

"Verify."

"How do I do that? The moment I start asking around about you, there's going to be a shitstorm coming toward me."

I lean down, reaching for my shoe.

The Pro pulls a weapon, so fast that his arm is a blur.

"Easy," he says.

I move slowly, taking off my shoe and pulling out the flash drive filled with files Howard stole from The Program server at the Mercurio Institute.

"What do you have there?" the mayor says.

"It's a flash drive," I say. "You'll find files downloaded directly from my organization yesterday."

I offer him the drive.

"You made your fortune in the computer-security industry, sir. There's enough on the drive to verify that The Program exists."

I'm hoping it's enough, because I don't know exactly what Howard pulled off The Program server.

"I'll take a look," the mayor says.

I say, "You have to cut any connection to the Web before you do it."

"My system is secure," the mayor says.

"There's no such thing," I say. "The Program has a network of child hackers spread across the country. If you're connected to the outside world, they can find you."

"You want me to shut down the power because of kids with computers?"

"Believe me, these are not regular kids. Shut it all down—phones, security systems, house automation. Anything that connects to the Web."

"Convenient," the Pro says. "If you were planning to attack the mayor, you'd want all the connections severed. No connection, no way to call for help."

"Lock me in," I say. "Tie me up. Do whatever you need to do to feel safe."

The mayor and the Pro look at each other, a decision passing between them.

"Give me the flash drive," the mayor says.

I hand it over to him.

"This is going to take a while," he says. "Make yourself comfortable. There are snacks and drinks in the bar."

"Thank you."

He gestures to the Pro, and they both head to the door.

The mayor says, "I'll take a look at what's on this drive, Zach. And I'll think seriously about what you've told me. I promise you that much."

"Thank you, sir."

"If I believe your story, I'll have the people who matter here in a few hours. We'll sort this out with them in a way that will ensure our safety."

The mayor opens the door, but he pauses before leaving and turns to me.

"I've missed you, Ben."

Before I can correct him, he adds, "I know that isn't your real name, but that's always how I'll think of you."

A flood of memories from New York comes rushing back, threatening to overwhelm me.

"I've missed you, too, sir."

The mayor nods once, then leaves the room. The Pro hesitates before following him out the door.

"I'm not restraining you," he says. "But I'm damn well locking you in."

He throws me a half salute, then he goes out and closes the door behind him. It clicks shut with a solid thud.

IT'S DONE.

I've told my story. It's out of my hands now.

If there's enough information on the flash drive, it will pique the mayor's interest and he'll follow it wherever it leads. If he takes the next step, I can ask him to bring Howard and Tanya into the house, make sure they're safe, and use them to back up my story.

And, finally, with the mayor's help, I'll find my father.

I try the door. It's locked, just as the Pro promised.

That's not a surprise.

A few minutes later the lights flicker, then go off. After a couple of seconds, an emergency generator kicks in and a set of alternate lights come on, bathing the room in a red glow. The main power supply to the mansion has been shut down. That means the mayor took my recommendations seriously, and he's studying the flash drive.

I begin to pace the room. I think about Tanya and Howard outside waiting for me. It's been over an hour since I left them. I'm trusting Tanya to keep Howard safe and, if need be, to make the decision to leave the area without me.

I drink the rest of the Coke and eat some trail mix I find on the bar. My body is depleted, and once I've eaten, exhaustion creeps into my bones.

I spend some time thinking about Mike in the backyard of the house earlier today, his gun trained on us. He should have finished the job and killed us, but he ran off after he saw that Tanya had turned against The Program. It was a short time later that The Program burned me in the media.

Did Mike say something to Mother that caused her to write me off?

I try to imagine what I would have done in Mike's situation, but I can't quite get my head around it.

My body feels heavy, the gravity of what I've done overtaking me.

I look down at the bar and see a decorative lighter with JG embossed on the side.

JG. Jonathan Goldberg. The mayor's lighter.

I study it up close, wondering who might have given it to him. I remember he enjoys a secret cigarette now and again when he's working. Samara hated that he smokes. She'd yell at him to stop, and her father would hide it from her, smoking in his study with the door locked and the windows open so he wouldn't upset her.

I wonder what it's like for him now that she's gone, smoking without being bothered, without anyone around to worry about him.

Suddenly I feel very tired, and I sink into the sofa where the mayor sat earlier. The fabric smells of his cologne, a scent that is as familiar as home.

I try to get up from the sofa, but I cannot. I breathe deeply, increasing the flow of oxygen to my brain, attempting to stay awake.

It doesn't work.

Eventually I can't fight it anymore. My eyes close, and I drift into a deep sleep.

THE SOUND OF THE DOOR WAKES ME.

My eyes snap open, and I find the lights back on in the mansion, the power restored. Mayor Goldberg strides into the room with the Pro at his side.

"We examined the flash drive," the Pro says. "Very compelling."

Something is off in his tone. I sense it immediately.

"You believe me?" I ask.

I look at the mayor, but he won't meet my eye.

"We did believe you," the Pro says. "Enough to take the next step."

"What's the next step?"

"I've got a relationship at the NSA. A woman I went to college with. It's a long story that my wife never tires of using against me. But with the mayor's permission, I gave the woman a call."

"The NSA doesn't know anything about what I do."

"Correct. She did not know you and, quite frankly, she found the whole story of The Program ridiculous. But I didn't stop there. I ran your prints."

"You got them off the thumb drive," I say, realizing what has happened.

"You touched it. I figured why not use what we have."

I should have given this guy more credit, but the prints won't have helped him. My true identity has been erased for a long time.

"So you ran my prints," I say. "And you didn't get any hits."

"On the contrary. Your name is Daniel Martin. You're from New Jersey."

"I'm not Daniel Martin."

The mayor steps forward. "I think your name is Daniel Martin," he says, "and I think you would know that under normal circumstances, but things might be a little confusing right now because you're off your meds."

"What are you talking about?" I say.

"Your parents reported you missing nine months ago, Daniel. It sounds like you guys were having problems. I'm sorry to hear it. I think you ran away and got involved with those crazies in New Hampshire. Maybe you knew what you were getting into, maybe you didn't. It's too late for regrets now."

"You've got it wrong," I say.

The Pro says, "Your mother told us you'd say that."

"My mother?"

"I turned on the iPhone," the mayor says. "And almost immediately I got a call from a very worried woman. She said you're being treated for bipolar disorder. Does that sound familiar?"

"I'm not bipolar."

"But you are familiar with the condition, Daniel?"

"My name is not Daniel."

"It's characterized by delusions of grandeur, paranoid conspiracy theories, manic behavior followed by long depressive episodes. It made you particularly susceptible to bad people who wanted to manipulate you."

"I know what bipolar disorder is, but I don't suffer from it."

"Enough," the mayor says.

He steps in and looks me in the eyes.

"Even with all that evidence against you, even after I spoke to your mother, I was willing to give you the benefit of the doubt. The documents on the flash drive seemed real and they had been encrypted with some of the most sophisticated security layers I've seen."

Score one for Howard.

The mayor says, "So I considered the out-of-the-box possibility that the evidence against you was falsified. Perhaps you were being framed, that an organization as powerful as you claim this one is would be capable of setting a deep-cover trap to discredit you."

"I appreciate you believing in me, sir."

The mayor's face goes slack.

"And then I received this," he says.

He takes out an iPad. He holds the tablet out to me and presses Play on a video.

I recognize the images of Central Park at night, a statue called Cleopatra's Needle visible in the glow of a full moon.

A shiver goes down my back.

The mayor drops the tablet on the coffee table in front of me, then he backs up.

I pick it up and watch the video.

A figure stands in the plaza in Central Park. The camera pulls in for a close-up.

It's me.

There is a woman lying at my feet.

Samara, the mayor's daughter.

I know this scene because I lived it. It's the last night I saw Samara after the firefight at Gracie Mansion. I chased her and confronted her in the park.

I've played the moment over and over in my head.

Now I watch it on the mayor's iPad.

"Who sent you this file?" I ask the mayor.

"Does it matter?" he says. "I know it's you and I know that's Samara with you. Do you deny it?"

I look at the video.

"It's us," I say.

There is no sound in the video, but I can clearly see Samara is alive at my feet. She is saying something to me.

I remember her words that night. She was begging for her life.

On the screen, I watch myself remove a weaponized pen from my pocket.

I kneel down next to Samara, and I press the point into her neck.

It takes only a few moments for her to stop moving.

"You killed my daughter," the mayor says. The cords in his neck are pulled tight with rage. "You killed my daughter, and you come to my home asking me for help."

"Mr. Mayor, please hear me out—"

I look at the Pro. He's drawn his weapon.

The mayor says, "Some people would say you're sick and, because of that, you're not responsible for your actions. But that's not how I see it."

The video ends, loops back to the beginning, and starts again.

I look at the style of video, the proportion of the clip.

It was shot from a camera phone.

Mike's phone.

After I completed my mission that night in Central Park, I looked up, startled to find a police officer had been watching me.

It was not a real cop. It was Mike, disguised as an NYPD officer.

Mike shot this video. And he sent it to the mayor tonight.

I think of Mike in the backyard earlier today. Before he disappeared, he told me that none of my friends had survived a mission. Except the mayor of New York.

Mike put this idea in my head.

He knew I would think of the mayor. He knew I would reach out to him for help.

He led me here, and I walked right into his trap.

The mayor says, "You may be sick, Daniel, but you are responsible. And you will be punished. So help me, God, I will see you punished for what you have done to me and my family."

The Pro opens the doors to the den. Almost two dozen FBI agents are there. They pour into the room, weapons at the ready. More agents fill the hallway behind them.

"Stay where you are," the lead FBI agent says.

The agents nearest me have drawn Tasers.

"Let's do this the easy way," the lead agent says.

The mayor says, "You have to go with these men, Daniel. If you cooperate, you won't be harmed."

He's wrong about that. I will be harmed. Maybe not by these men. But by the men that come after them. Or the ones after that.

"My name is not Daniel," I say, but the mayor is not listening to me anymore.

The agents advance.

I map the room. I can see twenty men. Four Tasers, sixteen automatic weapons. Probably countless more spread throughout the house and beyond.

The mayor is still in the room, too close to me for his own safety.

Four quick moves and I could take him hostage and use him to get out of the building.

But then I think about Howard and Tanya down the street. Even if I made it outside, I couldn't help them, not with a high-value hostage and FBI agents surrounding me.

I'd be on the run again, now with one of the most recognizable men in the world, and with every law enforcement officer on the planet out to find me.

If I allow myself to be arrested now, these agents will take me away and the manhunt ends.

That means Howard and Tanya will get a head start. They will have a chance.

"He's going to fight," the lead agent says to his team.

"I'm not going to fight," I say.

I relax my shoulders. I extend my arms in front of me, surrendering.

The agents rush in, quickly cuffing my arms and legs. They duckwalk me out to the hallway.

The mayor looks away, unwilling to meet my eye.

Four EMTs wait with an ambulance stretcher in the hall. They are surrounded by a precinct's worth of police officers lining the halls of the mansion.

The agents uncuff and recuff me to the metal bars of the stretcher. Another opportunity for escape passes by without my acting on it.

One of the EMTs checks me over, a quick assessment.

"You're dehydrated," he says, "and you seem to have some injuries. Were you in an accident?"

I nod.

"I'm going to start an IV to replenish your fluids."

"No needles," I say.

"Not an option," he says.

I jerk my arm and feel the cuffs tight on both sides.

Automatic weapons cock all around me.

I watch helplessly as the needle slides into my vein. I trace its path up a tube to a hanging bag that reads SODIUM CHLORINE INJECTION. A standard saline drip. At least that's what it looks like.

I yank at the cuffs again, checking for weak areas in the bars on the gurney. I don't find any.

"You don't want to break the needle off in your arm," the EMT says. "I'll have to dig it out, and it will hurt."

I keep fighting, pulling at the cuffs and rattling the gurney.

"I'm going to give you something to relax you," the EMT says.

Before I can object, he plunges a syringe into the tubing.

The drug works fast. My muscles unwind. I'm already lying down, but it feels like the gurney just got a lot softer beneath me. They've probably injected me with a high dose of lorazepam.

The stretcher starts to move through the halls of the mansion, accompanied by a massive circle of FBI agents.

After being on high alert for several days in a row, my body is exhausted. I fight to keep my eyes open, but the vibration of the wheels on the floor and the gentle rocking of the gurney are too much for me.

Suddenly we are outside. A cheer goes up from the baseball game. I crane my neck and see the crowd at the game standing, folding up their chairs, packing to go home. The game is over. I try to locate Howard and Tanya among the crowd, but I cannot find them.

Dozens of police vehicles line the road, their lights throwing eerie red shadows into the night.

I imagine Howard and Tanya watching me from across the street, powerless to do anything. They will get away and take care of each other. I'm sure of it.

Another wave of exhaustion washes over me. I snap my wrist against the cuffs, hear the sound of metal grinding against metal.

"You're going to hurt yourself," the EMT says.

I fight some more. The EMT sighs.

"Why do I always get the head cases?" he asks no one in particular.

I look around for the cops, hoping to explain things to them, but they are walking back to their patrol cars, leaving me in the hands of the EMTs. A motorcade is forming to lead the ambulance to the hospital.

Dark clouds start to spin above me.

"What did you give me?" I ask the EMT, because lorazepam alone should not put me out like this. The EMT doesn't answer, instead sliding me into the back of the ambulance and closing the door with a solid thud.

A bus. That's what EMTs call their vehicle. I'm in the back of the bus.

A children's song weaves its way through my head, voices singing about bus wheels turning. It's a song I remember from long ago.

I listen to it for a while before I realize it's my own voice I hear. I'm singing a song my father used to sing to me long ago.

"Time for beddie bye," one of the EMTs says, and he flips off the lights in the back of the ambulance.

The song gets louder, the melody slowing until it seems to echo around me.

"Do you hear that?" I say.

My father is singing to me now, his voice gentle, lulling me to sleep.

"He's hallucinating," an EMT says.

Everything I've done, everything I've tried to do. None of it has mattered. I can't help myself now, and there's nothing I can do to help Howard and Tanya. The mission to find and save my father has failed.

I have failed.

THE BEEPING OF A HEART MONITOR PULLS ME TOWARD CONSCIOUSNESS.

I'm in a surgical suite, surrounded by doctors in scrubs and masks looking down at me.

"Another ten-cc dose," a woman's voice says. "He's waking up."

An anesthesiologist puts a mask over my face. I try to resist, but my limbs aren't working.

A sheet is pulled from my chest. Betadine is swabbed across my shoulder in the area of my scar. A doctor leans over and probes at the scar with gloved hands.

"This looks painful," she says.

There's something familiar about her voice. I look at the set of eyes above the mask. Attractive eyes.

It's Dr. Acosta, The Program doctor who examined me before my last mission.

But how could that be? What is she doing in a hospital in Saratoga Springs?

She picks up a scalpel and moves it toward my chest.

I try to fight back, wake myself from what I'm sure is a nightmare. But the anesthesia will not allow it. As the scalpel blade descends, I slip down into blackness.

I FEEL THE WARMTH OF THE SUN ON MY FACE.

I open one eye, close it quickly against the light streaming through the blinds.

I remember it was night when they took me to the hospital.

It's daytime now. The next day? The next month?

"Is the sun bothering you?" a woman says.

A moment later the blinds are closed, and the sun is gone.

I open my eyes again. I see the white panels of a hospital drop ceiling above me. I note movement at the foot of the bed. A woman sits across from me, her chair pulled back against the wall so she can watch me.

It's Mother.

I blink hard, wondering if I'm dreaming.

I try to speak, but my throat is too dry.

"There's water next to you in the blue cup," she says.

I reach for it. I am no longer tied down, my movement restricted in any way. The cool water soothes my throat.

"Slowly," Mother says. "You'll choke on it."

I finish the water in five gulps. Refill the cup and drink again.

I sit up in bed.

"You've been on quite an adventure," Mother says.

I rub my eyes. This is not a dream. Mother is right here dressed in slacks and a white blouse, a suit jacket slung casually over the back of her chair.

I sort through the events from the time I walked into the mayor's mansion, up until the arrival of the FBI, followed by the ambulance driving me to the hospital.

I think of Tanya and Howard, waiting down the street at the baseball field.

Did they get away?

"They are safe," Mother says, as if she can read my thoughts.

"They?"

"Tanya and Howard. I imagine you're wondering about them," Mother says. "After all, you risked everything for them. I'm assuming there was a reason."

I'm trying to find the right thing to say, searching for my next move.

"No games, Zach. I'm putting my cards on the table. I expect you to do the same."

"Where are they?" I say.

"They're alive," Mother says.

I feel relieved, but I don't express it to Mother. Instead, I adjust my position so I can see her better. As I move, I feel a pain deep in my chest.

I reach up and explore the area with my fingers. There's a bandage, under which I feel stitches, tightly closing the wound over my scar.

A sensation passes through me, constricting my chest.

Fear.

"Was I operated on?" I say.

"In a manner of speaking," Mother says. "A previous procedure was reversed."

Mother holds up a plastic specimen container. She shakes it. Something rattles against the sides.

"What is it?"

She tosses it to me. I look at the familiar device in the bottom of the container.

"My chip," I say.

"Our chip, technically. It was on loan to you. We've taken back possession."

"What did you replace it with?"

"Nothing," she says. "We took out the chip, washed and closed the wound. You'll still have a scar, but it won't be any worse than before. You can have a plastic surgeon evaluate it in a few months."

"I'm confused," I say. "Why would you take out the chip?"

"For one thing, it had been tampered with."

I put the specimen container next to the bed.

I sip at my drink. Mother is running this show. I would be wise to slow down, let her lead the conversation, and listen closely.

"Am I mistaken about that?" she says. "The tampering?"

"No."

"How did you find out about the device?" Mother asks.

The chip's existence was supposed to be a secret to me. There's no reason to lie about it now.

"Francisco explained it to me," I say.

Francisco, the Beta agent, the second of five Program assassins. He had disappeared, and I was sent to complete his mission.

"You met Francisco?" Mother says.

Her tone is relaxed, but she sits up straight in the chair, her posture belying her true feelings.

"He was still alive when I got inside Moore's compound."

"You didn't tell us."

"There are many things we didn't tell each other," I say, touching my chest.

"He was a traitor, wasn't he?" Mother says.

"Yes."

I see Mother's hand clench into a fist.

"And you, Zach. Are you a traitor?"

I consider the question.

"It depends on your definition," I say.

Mother stands up slowly, slips her suit jacket on.

"Get dressed," she says. "You'll find clothes that fit you in the closet."

"Where are we going?" I ask.

"I want to show you something."

I don't know what Mother is up to, but my best move is to go along until I understand better.

I get out of bed, testing the strength in my legs and stretching to activate sore muscles. I'm stronger, my nutrients replenished, my body rested from the trials of the last few days.

"How long have I been here?" I say.

"Two days. We've been feeding you intravenously to give your body time to heal."

I open the closet door. I find jeans, a T-shirt, and a leather jacket laid out on a shelf along with underwear.

Mother turns her back to give me privacy. By doing so, she leaves herself open to attack.

It might be a test; it might be a demonstration of faith.

I have the advantage, but I don't act on it.

Once I'm dressed, Mother opens the door and steps back, inviting me to walk through ahead of her. The skin on the back of my neck tingles.

I am in danger. I can feel it.

Mother senses my trepidation. She says, "If I wanted to kill you, I would have done it already."

"There are things worse than death," I say.

"What could be worse?" Mother says.

I don't answer. I don't have to.

I walk through the door.

I'M NOT IN A HOSPITAL.

It's obvious as soon as I step out the door, into a long, carpeted hallway lined with ornate wooden panels. Mother directs me down the hall, out into the bright sunshine of a small campus.

"What is this place?" I ask.

"It used to be a university," Mother says. "We've adapted it for our own use."

"We?"

"The Program," Mother says. "This is our new training academy."

She guides me to a vista between two buildings and points at a farmhouse about a half mile away.

"Do you recognize that place?"

I study the farmhouse. The design is familiar, as is the color of the paint on the wooden shingles.

"That's where it began," I say.

Mother nods.

I'm looking at the training house where I was taken by Mike

when I was twelve years old. It was in that house that I had my first experience of The Program.

"We've all grown up since then," Mother says. "I need these damn glasses now."

She takes eyeglasses from a case and slides them on. I recognize the same glasses I saw during our video call the other day.

I look back at the campus around us. "This is The Program?"

She nods. "The farmhouse, this campus. You've come home, Zach."

The doors of a building fly open across the quadrangle, and children stream out, backpacks flung over their shoulders. I see kids as young as seven or eight, others in their midteens. As they pass by, the kids acknowledge Mother with deferential nods and set faces, no smiles. A few of them steal glances at me, then look away quickly, their postures stiff and focused.

"We've been up and running here for about eighteen months," Mother says.

"Are the kids recruits?"

"They're being trained much like you were. We've had to adjust the process, of course, to deal with the greater numbers."

"Where are they from?"

"Some of them are street kids, some orphans, others the byproduct of Program operations like yourself," Mother says. "But wherever they come from, we are their family now."

I look at the young faces passing by. I think about the risks inherent in training so many kids, divulging the secrets of The Program to recruits who might not make it through the coursework.

"What happens if they don't graduate?" I ask.

If Mother lets any of these kids go, they take the secrets of The Program with them.

"Our goal is to make sure everyone graduates," she says. "If there is failure, it means we have failed. It's on us, not them."

She's looking right at me as she says it.

"What you see is only the tip of the iceberg," Mother says. She points to a massive building with an arched roof on our right. "Let me give you a tour."

WE STEP INTO A LARGE, EMPTY GYMNASIUM.

Almost empty.

Because a girl is stretching out on a mat on the far side of the gym. She cracks her neck and readjusts her position, executing a series of powerful kicks, her leg traveling ever higher as she maintains her balance on one foot.

She stops when she sees us. Mother waves her over, and she trots toward us.

The moment she turns, I know who it is.

Tanya.

It takes me a second to process what I'm seeing, but just a second.

Tanya is the Gamma agent. She was always the Gamma. I was a fool to believe differently.

She walks up to us wearing workout tights and a small T-shirt that accentuates her body. Her bearing is different, relaxed but authoritative.

I say, "Everything that happened between us—it was an act?"

Her expression remains passive.

"Isn't that what we do, Zach? We act. We play a role."

"Not all of us. I was trying to keep you alive."

"You're lying to yourself. You didn't really care about me. You were working out some kind of misplaced guilt for past missions. You made yourself feel better by being vulnerable for a little while and doing a good deed for a couple of kids. If you really cared about us, you would have dropped us off at the first police station. Put us in the hands of the authorities."

"That wouldn't have protected you. Not from The Program."

"Who was the prime target? You or us?"

She's right.

The Program was after me, not them. I should have dropped them off, gotten them away from me and into the hands of people who could help them. But I didn't. Why?

Tanya and Mother trade glances. Tanya says, "You kept what you thought were two innocent kids with you, when you were the target. I had heard so much about the famous Zach Abram, I wanted to see how you worked in the field. Well, I saw what I needed to see. You're selfish and, worse, you're dangerous. I watched that helicopter go down with Father in it—"

Mother stiffens next to me.

Tanya blinks. She noticed it, too.

Tanya lowers her voice. "I saw Father die, and maybe it wasn't your fault directly. So I gave you the benefit of the doubt, at least until you went to the mayor. But when push came to shove, you were more than willing to destroy The Program. That's when I understood that you would sacrifice anything to get what you wanted. Your friend Howard. Mother. The Program. Me. None of us really mattered to you. The only thing you cared about was finding your father."

"That's not true, Tanya."

"We have a code. Primary objective: Protect The Program. Secondary objective: Survive. You're very good at the second, but you seem to have forgotten the first. You came damn close to destroying everything we've built here. Thank God Mike stopped you."

She knows about the video he sent to the mayor.

I look at Tanya, her jaw set tight, her eyes defiant.

A few days ago I thought I loved this girl. Now I know I was wrong. My feelings have betrayed me again.

Sam, Miranda, Tanya.

Mike was right. Every time I let my feelings guide me, I make mistakes, and people get hurt. Now I've made the biggest mistake of all, and innocent people are going to suffer for it.

"What happened to Howard?" I ask.

"I turned him over to The Program," Tanya says, her voice cold.

I look at her and my face burns with shame.

"You had me fooled," I say. "Why didn't you kill me? You had plenty of opportunity."

She looks to Mother for permission to speak.

"Tell him," Mother says.

"I was following orders," Tanya says with a shrug.

"What was your mission?"

"Get close, report, and keep you alive."

"Keep me alive?"

"Ironic, isn't it? You thought you were the one keeping me alive," she says, "but it was the other way around. I was making sure nothing happened to you, because The Program wanted you back."

I race through my memories of the days since I broke into the holding house. So much has happened between Tanya and me. Could it all have been part of a plan?

Mother watches my face. "Naturally, you'll have questions," she says. She turns back to Tanya. "Thank you for your hard work."

"My pleasure, ma'am."

I look into Tanya's eyes. I don't see the girl I thought I knew.

I see a soldier. Cold, calculating, dangerous.

Tanya walks across the gymnasium, returning to her workout mat. She doesn't look back.

Mother gestures to the doors. "Let's talk outside," she says.

Child soldiers walk side by side across the quad in front of me, their cadence perfectly in sync.

Mother joins me a moment later.

"Where is Howard?" I ask.

"We have him. We're questioning him, making sure we understand the full nature of his involvement with you."

I imagine Howard being tortured somewhere on this campus where I cannot get to him.

"Why don't you question me instead? I'll tell you anything you want to know."

"You'll tell us and he'll tell us. Then we'll compare the stories. You know that's the only way."

I clench my fists, trying to keep myself from doing or saying anything that might put Howard at greater jeopardy.

"Why did you take me into the gym, Mother?"

"I wanted you to know the truth."

"What truth? That I'm fallible? That I can be fooled so easily by an agent?"

"I wanted you to know that my goal was to keep you alive. I did everything in my power to do so."

"If you were trying to keep me alive, why was Mike trying to kill me?"

Mother's eyelid flutters, but just barely. It's enough to suggest she might be surprised by what I've said. But she recovers quickly.

"Perhaps it seemed like he was trying to kill you, but I would suggest that he was several steps ahead of you, leading you where he wanted you to go."

"Like walking a dog."

Mother shrugs. "Your words, not mine. For my part, I was trying to bring you back to us by any means necessary. I did so at great expense to The Program. I don't need to remind you of that, do I? Of the losses we've suffered because of you?"

She closes her eyes, and a pained expression crosses her face.

"Terrible losses," she says. "But not insurmountable ones."

She opens her eyes and looks at me.

"The Program is not one person," Mother says. "Nobody can be more important than the organization. Not Father, not me. The Program comes first and foremost."

"Protect The Program."

"Your first objective, and mine."

"If the objective is to protect The Program, why did you release my image to the media? The whole world knows my face as the face of a terrorist."

Mother starts down the steps.

"Perhaps that was an overreaction," Mother says. "I regret it, but it was not my call."

Whose call could it have been? Who is more powerful than Mother?

"The good news is faces can be changed," she says. "As can stories in the media. Mistakes happen all the time."

Mother begins to walk, gesturing for me to follow her.

"We'll find a way to make it right," Mother says. "That is, if you decide to stay with us."

I look at her, surprised.

"It's time for you to make a choice about The Program, Zach."

"A choice? That's a novel idea."

I think of the farmhouse not too far from here. That first day with The Program.

Join us or die. That's what Mother said.

"You were a child then. You can't give a child real choices. They're not capable of understanding them. But you're not a child anymore, are you?"

"No," I say.

"Today is the day you decide whether you're going to stay with us."

"I can be a part of The Program again? Even after all that's happened?"

"Mike and I have talked a lot about it. He tells me young men have growing pains and we have to allow for that. If The Program doesn't learn to flex, it will break. That's Mike's opinion. He's urged me to flex in your case."

"So you would put me back on assignment?"

"Eventually, yes."

"And if I choose not to stay?"

"You'd be free to forge your own path. If you check your bank balance, you'll find five hundred thousand dollars in the account, a onetime payment you can use to resettle yourself, go to college, whatever you choose to do. We've removed your chip, so we have our property back. We will arrange a new, clean identity for you to start over."

"Others have left before me?"

Mother shakes her head. "You'd be the first."

"Why me?"

She smiles like she's been waiting for this moment. "You already know the answer, don't you?"

"My father helped to create The Program."

She nods, indicating the campus with widespread arms.

"Everything around us. It's all because of him. If you choose to leave, you're on your own. If you stay—then it's time for you to learn the truth about your father."

"Is he alive?" I ask.

"Alive and well."

"Mike told me he was dead. Tanya said he was a prisoner."

"Mike was not authorized to tell you the truth. And Tanya does not know the truth."

"If my father's alive, I want to see him. I want proof."

"He wants to see you, too. After all, you're the soldier who carries his name."

"I'm his son."

"His son is a soldier. If you choose to stay a soldier, you can meet him."

"This is a trick," I say.

"No trick," Mother says. "Common sense. It's for our protection and yours."

"If my father is alive, he would want to see me whether I was a soldier or not."

"He hasn't seen you in five years, has he? He's been alive that whole time."

"That's because you've imprisoned him!" I say.

"You think you know the real story, but you have no idea."

I breathe deeply, trying not to react to Mother's provocation. I've had this same thought a thousand times. If my father were alive, he would have come for me. He would have communicated somehow. He would have tried to save me.

Mother gestures to an ivy-covered building across the way from us.

"What's your choice going to be?" Mother says.

"I'll do anything to meet my father," I say.

Mother smiles.

"Welcome back to The Program," she says. "You'll find your father inside."

I take a step toward the building. My mind rebels, shouting for me to turn back. It's the same intuition that keeps me safe on missions, the part of me that reacts to threats before they are revealed.

So why is it warning me now?

I set the warning aside and keep moving forward.

A large wooden door fronts the entrance. There is a keypad in the wall of the building, the telltale holes for a laser-detection system bored into the wood frame. This old building has been retrofitted with high-tech security.

I reach out and turn the door handle.

It's unlocked.

I STEP INSIDE.

The air is heavy with the smell of old wood. I am facing a long, dark hallway with a glimmer of light at the far end.

I head for it.

There are signs of technology embedded everywhere, tiny camera lenses at intervals in the moldings, the telltale click of pressure plates triggered beneath the carpet as I walk.

A door is open at the end of the hall. A man sits at a large mahogany table across the room studying a computer screen in front of him.

He looks up as I step into the room. I blink hard and rub my eyes.

This man is my father.

He is older, and he's lost weight. But there's no question of his identity.

He stands when he sees me. "My God," he says.

I rub my face and my fingers come away wet. I'm crying.

I haven't cried since I was a child.

"Is it really you?"

"It's me," my father says.

There are tears in his eyes, too.

We rush toward each other, meeting in the middle of the room in a tight embrace.

"How long has it been?" he says.

I step away from him.

"I thought you were dead," I say. "You've been working with The Program the whole time?"

"Yes," he says.

His energy changes, and he becomes nervous, shifting from side to side on the balls of his feet.

I lower my voice. "Are they holding you hostage?"

He gives me a sad smile.

"Oh, Zach. We have a lot to talk about, don't we?"

"You didn't answer my question."

"I'm not a hostage. I'm not here against my will."

"I don't understand—did you know that I was searching for you?"

"I knew."

"Why didn't you come for me?" I say.

He leans forward, looking me in the eye.

"I knew that you were a soldier and that you were on assignment. It wasn't my place to interfere, so I watched you from the sidelines."

I feel anger clench in my throat.

"You couldn't interfere, or you didn't want to?"

"It hurt me not to communicate with you, but those were the rules."

"Whose rules?"

He takes a deep breath. "I'll tell you everything you want to know," he says.

He sits down at a long table and invites me to sit across from him.

"I heard you met Dr. Silberstein a few days ago."

"That's right," I say.

"How is that old bastard?"

I think of the professor splayed on the ground, a gunshot to his head.

"He's been better," I say.

"He thinks I died in a car accident a long time ago, and he took over our research. He won, and I lost. I'm sure that makes him very happy."

That jibes with Silberstein's story of a rivalry between partners.

"Why doesn't he know the truth?" I ask.

"We had to create a firewall around The Program, and he's on the outside. His research is vitally important to us, but he can't know how it's being used."

"How is it being used?"

My father points to my chest.

"The chip," he says.

"He invented the neurosuppressor chip?"

"Silberstein? He's not capable of that," my father says.

That's when I realize what my father is trying to tell me.

"It was you," I say.

My father claps his hands, delighted.

"I didn't know you were an inventor," I say. "Silberstein told me you were studying post-traumatic stress disorder when I was a kid."

My father leaps up and leans over the table, suddenly excited. "That's right," he says. "There was a great rush to that subject matter after the wars in Iraq and Afghanistan. Many of our young soldiers came back with psychological issues. The fear they experienced during deployment was so powerful, it imprinted itself into the bio-chemistry of their brains."

My father paces through the lab, getting more agitated as he speaks.

"I watched countless soldiers suffer, their lives forever diminished by their service. It made me angry, Zach. Why should a nine-month deployment lock people into hell for the rest of their lives? One day it occurred to me that our approach was wrong. We were treating the damage after the fact rather than preventing it in the first place. I realized that no matter how soon we got to the soldiers, the damage had already been done. All because of fear. But if I could prevent the fear from taking hold—"

"That's what the chip does. It removes fear."

"We installed the prototype in the first group of soldiers, and their performance improved as they became free of fear on the battlefield, but those improvements quickly disappeared."

"The chip didn't work?" I say.

My father looks troubled, scratching his head.

"It seemed to be working, yet the soldiers became fearful again and started to experience PTSD. Even though these young men were not feeling fear on the battlefield, they were *remembering* fear they had experienced earlier in their lives. In a sense, their brains knew they were supposed to be afraid—"

"So they were using old fears to replace the fear they weren't feeling during battle."

"Precisely. By the time we implanted the chip, the soldiers already had a memory base of fear. The soldiers were young, but they weren't young enough."

"You needed children," I say.

My father nods. "Children raised on war movies and video games. They'd never experienced the repercussions of violence, so it was fun to them. If we could keep them in that place, they would be free during battle. They would become supersoldiers, and the risk of PTSD would be eradicated."

I reach up to the scar on my chest, think about the secret surgery that put the chip in my body many years ago.

My father says, "This is where Mother's stroke of genius came in. She was our contact at the Department of Defense, and when I told her what I had discovered, she was inspired. The chip worked best if it was implanted in children twelve or younger, but we couldn't send twelve-year-olds to war, and it wasn't reasonable to wait six or eight years for them to become old enough to join the military. Besides, Mother said we needed them here at home, doing a job that nobody else could do."

"Instead of making them soldiers, you made them assassins."

"It was the birth of The Program," my father says. "Can you see the brilliance of the idea? The Program was the perfect modality to test the chip."

A wave of dizziness overtakes me. I reach out and steady myself against the table.

"And I was a part of that test," I say.

"You were one of the first. Not the very first, because I wouldn't do that to you, son. I was able to refine the chip through several generations, and when I thought I'd gotten close to perfect, it was time."

"Time for me to join The Program."

He leans forward, reaching out to grasp my forearm.

"You asked me why I couldn't communicate with you these last few years. I know it hurt you. I know you suffered. But I need you to understand that it wasn't my choice. *The experiment required it.* You had to believe you were orphaned so you would undergo the training. Then we could see how the chip functioned in the field."

"I'm the experiment?"

"Not *the* experiment. *My* experiment."

I get up and walk around the lab. I see stacks of narrow drawers labeled with ID numbers.

"Mother had my chip removed two days ago," I say.

"I know," my father says. "I ordered her to remove it."

"You ordered her?"

My father turns toward me, locking his eyes on mine.

"I am The Program," he says. "I invented the technology, I put it into practice, and now I manage the assets. Mother works for me, Zach."

I can't believe what I'm hearing.

"You had the chip removed," I say. "Does that mean your experiment is over?"

My father clears his throat. "All experiments need refinement, Zach."

He licks his lips, then grabs for a pitcher of water on the table. He pours a glass and hungrily swallows it down.

"Rude of me," he says, and he pours a second glass and slides it toward me.

I don't touch it.

"This must be hard for you," my father says. "It's a lot to take in all at once."

"It's not hard for you?"

"For both of us. That's what I meant."

He purses his lips, looking at me with pity.

"None of this is your fault," he says. "Your rebellion the last few missions. Your moves against The Program. I take responsibility for all of it."

"What do you mean by that?"

"The chip was flawed. Not you, son."

My mouth goes dry. I reach for the water, drinking it in one long swallow.

"It was never you," my father says. "It was me."

He opens one of the narrow drawers and removes a metal tray. On the tray is a computer chip inset in yellow foam. He pulls on a glove, gently removes the chip, and holds it up for me to see.

"What is it?"

"It's the solution," he says. "Removing fear wasn't enough, because it's not just fear that cripples us. It's doubt. It's uncertainty. All of our emotions. You can be fearless, yet still be plagued by other emotional demons. You know what I mean, don't you?"

I think about Tanya in the gym earlier. The feeling of betrayal.

I remember New York, where my feelings for Samara led me to question my mission for the first time. That was the beginning of a long process that led me to this room.

"Feelings are a problem," I say.

My father nods. "Even Mike, the most loyal soldier of all, is still prone to certain—shall we say—indiscretions."

Does my father know what Mike has been up to?

My father reaches for a forceps. "Once this chip is inside you, there will be no more feelings. No questions, no mistakes, no need for disloyalty."

He uses the forceps to remove a plastic wrapping from around the chip.

"You are my greatest experiment, Zach. My greatest accomplishment. You deserve the best I can give you."

I suddenly understand.

"That's why you ordered Mother to remove my chip," I say.

"Yes," Father says. "You're getting an upgrade. Right now."

He pulls up a chair and wheels a light toward it.

"Remove your shirt and jacket," he says. He motions for me to sit.

Mother told me I had to make a choice. Take my chances alone in the world or rejoin The Program and be reunited with my father.

Now my father is in front of me, offering me the chance to become a great soldier again.

I unbutton my shirt.

My father comes toward me, close enough to smell.

I remember the fragrance of his cologne when I was riding on his shoulders as a kid. It was similar to the smell I experienced with the mayor.

I breathe deeply, expecting the familiar scent of my childhood, but I don't find it.

This man doesn't smell like my father anymore.

He runs his finger over the scar on my chest. I shiver at his touch.

"It will be a bit cold," my father says.

He swabs my chest with an antiseptic solution.

"I'm going to inject the area with some lidocaine to make it less painful. Unless you'd rather we knock you out completely?"

"I've been out enough in the last week. I want to be awake for this," I say.

He nods and drapes a blue sheet over my shoulder. There's a large hole in the center, exposing my scar to the air.

"I'll snip open the stitches and insert the chip, make sure it's powered up properly. Then I'll close the wound. It won't take more than ten minutes start to finish. There will be some pain—"

"I can handle pain," I say.

"I know you can."

Father takes a plastic pack from a tray. He tears it open and removes a syringe with a long needle. He removes the cap from the needle and pokes it through the top of a vial of lidocaine, preparing the injection for my chest.

"Will I remember?" I say.

He smiles. "The chip doesn't take away your memories."

"No?"

"Just your feelings. But I promise you will have a new perspective on things afterward. And a new ability to carry out your missions."

"I'm glad."

He smiles and pats my arm with a gloved hand.

"This will sting a little," he says. "At least until the lidocaine takes effect. Then you won't feel anything."

"Good," I say.

My voice sounds strange as it bounces off the stacks of books around us.

Father leans forward, pressing with one hand to find the proper injection point. With the other, he reaches toward me with the syringe.

I take his wrist, stopping him.

"One last question," I say.

"Of course."

"You haven't mentioned Mom at all," I say. "Not through this entire story you've told me."

"Your mother is gone," my father says.

"Where did she go?"

"She's dead."

I shiver. The air feels cold against my bare skin.

"How did she die?"

I let go of his wrist. He places the syringe on the tray.

"She disagreed with the way things were going. With the government contracts, the secrecy. And especially with you."

"She didn't like the experiment?" I say.

"She didn't want me to put the chip inside you. In fact, she forbade it."

"But you insisted," I say.

I notice sweat breaking out on his forehead. "She wouldn't listen, Zach. I tried to explain, to reason with her, but she was an unreasonable woman. I gave her the choice to leave. The DoD didn't want me to do it, but I convinced them that your mom could be trusted. I offered her a divorce, money, anything she wanted if she would leave and keep quiet."

"But she wouldn't leave."

"Not without you," he says. "The one thing I couldn't give her."

"So they killed her. You killed her."

My father stops, and his shoulders slump.

"I know you loved her, Zach. I loved her, too. But she was emotional, and she could have brought the entire Program down."

My mother was emotional. My father is rational, calculating.

I have all those qualities.

My father picks up the syringe again, sliding his chair toward me.

Once the chip is installed, there will be only one side.

"This is too much for you to take in all at once," my father says. "We can discuss it further once the procedure is done. I think you'll see things differently then."

A new chip will mean a chance to start again. Without feelings, and without remorse.

My father finds the proper insertion point with his right hand. I feel the prick of the needle in my chest.

He says, "We will have a lot of time to get reacquainted. I promise you."

"No, we won't," I say.

I reach up and grab his arm, pulling the needle out of me before he can depress the plunger.

He says, "What are you do—"

"I won't let you turn me into a machine," I say.

I wrench his arm away, and he fights me, struggling to complete the injection.

"Stop this, Zach."

"Mother said I had a choice."

"You have no choice," my father says.

He is stronger than he looks, fighting me for control of the syringe, attempting to force the needle into me.

"Just like the kids here didn't have a choice?" I say. "You're the only one who makes choices in this world."

"I know what's best for everyone," my father says. "Especially you, son."

"I don't think so," I say.

I grab his wrist with both hands, pull the needle up and away from my chest, twist it hard—

And plunge it into the vein on the side of his neck.

I depress the syringe quickly, injecting the lidocaine directly into his venous system.

As a local anesthetic, lidocaine is safe and effective as a numbing agent. But intravenously and in sufficient amounts, it is a cardiac depressant.

I know this from my training. So does Father, because the instant it happens, his eyes widen in shock and terror.

I step away from him.

Father clutches first at his neck, then at his chest. He spins around, rushing toward the medical supplies on the bench behind him. He stumbles before he gets there, going down to his knees, his hand striving to reach the shelf.

He looks back at me, his eyes pleading as he clutches his chest.

"Epinephrine," he whispers.

Epinephrine, also known as adrenaline. An epi injection would speed up his heart, stop the cardiac decline that is cascading inside him right now.

His face twists in agony.

A part of me wants to help him, to save his life.

I think about my mother, dying at the hands of The Program because she loved me too much to let me go. She risked everything to give me a chance to live a normal life.

I want that, too.

I look at my father as he makes one last grasp for the supplies, misses, and falls, rolling over onto his back, white foam forming at the corner of his lips. A sound like a growl comes from deep in his throat.

"I'm your father," he says.

"I remember my father. You're not the same man."

He struggles to maintain eye contact as he fights for breath. But the drug is too strong inside him. Eventually he gives in and his eyes begin to close.

I watch my father dying in front of me.

Dying for the second time. It will be the last time. I'm sure of it.

His chest heaves twice, three times. Then he is still.

The room is quiet. I look around at the equipment, the scribbled equations on whiteboards, the tech equipment covering the worktable. It looks like insanity to me.

I sit on the floor next to my father's lifeless body. I put a hand on his chest.

And I feel everything.

The man I loved in my childhood. The man who abandoned me and turned me into an experiment. The man I thought he was, and the one he turned out to be.

I think about him past and present.

And I say my final good-byes.

I should get up before someone comes, but my body is heavy with feeling. Eventually I fight my way to standing.

I have to get out of here. I have to find Howard.

Before I leave, I pick up the chip, my father's masterpiece and his final achievement.

I drop it to the floor in front of me. And I crush it under my heel.

MOTHER IS ALONE, WAITING FOR ME ACROSS THE CAMPUS LAWN.

She waves a greeting when she sees me, and we walk toward each other.

She scrutinizes me, perhaps sensing something is not right.

"Your father told you the story of The Program?" she says.

"All of it."

"He's an amazing man."

"He said you were the inspiration."

Mother says, "I'm grateful to have played a small part."

I make my face placid, blocking her from my true feelings.

"So it's done?" she says, touching her own chest in the same location where my chip was to be implanted.

"The surgery? Yes."

"How do you feel?"

"Different," I say.

"I have to admit, I was concerned when your father told me his plan. I didn't want us to do anything that might impair your performance, but he assured me this would be the best thing for you moving forward."

"Forward. I agree that's where our focus needs to be."

Mother's face softens. "It will take time for your new chip to fully engage. You may have to ride out some feelings for a while."

"What then?"

I can see that Mother is choosing her words carefully.

"Then they won't trouble you in the same way," she says.

I understand what Mother is saying. From her perspective, feelings interfere with the mission. They create problems like doubt, fear, and hesitation. I've experienced all of those things in the last few months.

If she wants to control the mission, she must control the feelings of her soldiers.

But I will not be controlled anymore.

We stroll together through the campus. It's a beautiful day, a blue, cloudless sky stretching above us. Some kids jog by at a clip, perhaps late for class.

A moment ago I killed my father, yet life goes on, stubbornly immune to tragedy.

I've seen this before on my missions. Now I'm experiencing it.

Mother stops at the edge of the campus, looking out at the residential neighborhoods far in the distance.

"Your father and I created a project that will change the world forever. How many people can say that about their work?"

I look at the houses laid out in neat rows in the valley below us. Normal people living normal lives, oblivious to the things The Program does here. What would they say if they knew the truth?

I think about Howard, a regular kid caught up in a secret world, all because of me. Maybe it was weakness that caused me to tell him about The Program back in New York. Maybe I was lonely and didn't know it.

Whatever my reason, it was a mistake.

"Where are we keeping Howard?" I say.

I use the pronoun *we*. Let Mother think I've chosen The Program. Maybe I can get Howard out of here before she finds out the truth.

"Why are you asking?" Mother says.

"He could be useful to us. He's a genius on the Web. He cracked The Program's server at my request. I doubt anyone has made it inside before. And if he could do that to us, he could do it for us."

"You want to recruit him," Mother says.

"I already recruited him. I just need to widen his perspective."

Mother smiles. I can see she is interested in the idea.

"He's in an interrogation cell. I'll take you there."

She turns away from the vista of the town, and I follow her back onto the quad.

"When you came to us in the beginning, Zach, it wasn't by choice. Your father and I wanted to make amends for that."

"Is that why you brought me back?" I say.

"We wanted to give you the opportunity to make the choice. As an adult."

"I've made it," I say.

At that moment, an alarm sounds through the campus, high-pitched bursts that echo across the stone walls. Children begin streaming out of the buildings around us, moving toward what appear to be assigned defensive positions around the campus.

Before Mother can say anything, Mike rushes toward us, accompanied by a small group of teens carrying automatic weapons.

"What's going on?" Mother says.

Mike ignores her, his gun aimed at my chest. "Step away from her," he says.

Mother turns to me, stunned.

I take slow steps back. The teens surround Mother, pulling her safely away from me.

I watch Mike. The normal calm of his features is gone, replaced by something dark and menacing.

"Dr. Abram is dead," he says to Mother.

"Oh my God," she says. She looks at me. "You killed your father?"

"I told you. I made my choice."

Mother's eyes grow cold. She types a code into her phone, and the alarm stops as thick metal poles rise out of the sidewalk around the perimeter of the campus.

They are crash barriers, preventing any vehicles from entering or exiting.

Mike says, "Get away from here, Mother. Let me deal with it."

She locks eyes with me for what seems like a long time. I can see she's making a decision. Finally, she breaks eye contact.

"Finish this," she says to Mike.

Then she hurries away, guarded on all sides by the teens.

Now Mike and I stand alone on the quad, facing each other.

"You stupid idiot," he says. "You killed the only person who cares about us in the world."

"He didn't care about anybody," I say.

"You're a liar!" he says, wiping snot from his nose. "He loved you. He always loved you, no matter how much you screwed up."

What is Mike talking about?

"No matter what I did or how impressive I was, it didn't matter. You were his son, and you were the favorite."

I've never seen Mike express emotion, but there's no hiding it now. He's distracted, his gun hand hanging at his side, the weapon no longer pointed at me. His face is red and blotchy, his eyelids puffy. That's when I realize:

Mike is jealous.

Something is dawning on me, some understanding of Mike's behavior that I didn't get before.

"Why did you tell me my father was dead?" I ask.

"What does it matter now?"

"You tried to kill me, too, or you seemed to be trying. But when you finally had the opportunity after Tanya stabbed you, you ran away."

"Why would I kill you," he says, "when it was better for you to kill yourself?"

"I don't understand. You wanted me to escape and go to the mayor?"

He chuckles and shakes his head.

"I was on your side for so long," Mike says. "I kept your secrets in New York and New Hampshire. I gave you every chance to be a part of The Program again, even when you had doubts, even when you screwed up. It took a long time, but I finally realized you were a lost cause. I could see it so clearly, but your father refused to see it. You were his son, and he was blind to your failings."

"Even after the helicopter crashed? Even after Father died?"

"You killed the third in command, but even that wasn't sufficient. Your father felt there were extenuating circumstances that led to the crash. He wanted you to be brought back and reprogrammed. That was the breaking point for me. I knew he would never see the truth. There was nothing I could tell him that would make him betray his bond with you. You were going to have to destroy that bond yourself."

His face is changing as he speaks, the grief receding, replaced by something dark and more familiar.

He says, "All the years I spent being the perfect soldier, and none of them mattered. Not compared with the bond of blood you shared. No matter what I did, I would always be the poor stepchild. So, you see, it wouldn't make sense for me to kill you. I needed you to kill yourself."

"Then you would be the favorite."

"That was the plan," he says. "But you destroyed any hope of that today."

Mike stares at me, seething. "You finally found your father," he says. "And you killed him."

"I found someone," I say. "He wasn't my father. Not anymore."

"That's convenient to think, isn't it? To take some of the guilt off you. You never had a stomach for killing. I should have known when you hesitated on that bitch in New York. You deviated from the mission, and I gave you a pass. So that's on me."

He steps sideways quickly. I counter with a step to the right.

He moves again, and I counter.

He smiles. "We've been doing this dance for five years," he says. "I'm tired of it."

"You and me both," I say.

Mike places the gun at his feet.

"I doubt I'm going to need this," he says as he assumes a combat fighting stance.

I tense my body, testing muscle groups in rapid succession. I am not at my best, but I am functional. That might be enough to take on Mike, or it might not. I won't know until it's over.

Mike moves to the left, dancing on his toes. I step back, putting a little more distance between us, letting him telegraph his moves to me if he will.

"Your father told you the truth, didn't he? How does it feel to know you're a laboratory animal? A testing subject."

His tone is mocking. He's trying to agitate me and throw me off my game. It's the same technique I've been taught. A psychological advantage can be more powerful than a physical one. So I retaliate.

"What about you, Mike? You're the Alpha. That means you were the first to get the chip. Did my father give you the upgrade? Or was that reserved for me alone?"

"I got the goddamn upgrade, you better believe I did. I've been a full generation ahead of you for a long time."

He pulls up his shirt. On one side I see the damage from Tanya's knife attack, neatly bandaged. On the other side there is a scar, much like the one on my chest, but his is just below the rib cage.

"My chip is under the ribs," he says. "More protection that way. The surgery hurt like hell, but that didn't stop me."

I slip off my jacket and open my shirt to reveal the stitches over my scar. "I lied to you, Mike. My chip is gone. They took it out."

"Bullshit," Mike says. "There is no you without the chip."

"It's gone and I'm still here," I say.

He shakes his head.

"You want to fight with a disadvantage, that's your prerogative," he says. "I'm going to do my thing either way. I've got a new legacy to build."

"What legacy is that?"

"I'll be the assassin who killed the assassin who tried to destroy our Program. That sounds alpha to me. Way fucking alpha."

Mike pulls a knife from his belt and waves it in the air. A glint of sun catches the blade on its deadly arc through the air.

He watches my reaction.

"You're afraid of knives, aren't you? At least since I stuck one into you on graduation."

He comes at me, the blade a liquid blur. I step back and dodge, but he slashes down and a cut opens on my forearm.

It happens so quickly, it takes several seconds for the pain to catch up to the strike.

I look at the ground and see spots of blood appearing on the asphalt by my feet.

Mike seizes the advantage, coming at me again.

I pick up my jacket and wind it around my forearm, the thick leather a shield against the blade.

"Nice move," he says.

"I don't need your approval."

"Times have changed, huh?"

He comes at me, the blade whistling in front of his body. He slashes at me from underneath and I parry, extending my forearm to take the strike. The knife slices through the leather with a whisper. But it does not make contact with my flesh.

He rushes in again, this time coming down from above, using gravity and inertia to slice at my arm. The blade makes contact with the jacket zipper, and sparks fly.

I back up and look at the jacket. There are two deep slices, the leather separating to reveal hints of fabric beneath.

One or two more strikes, that's all the jacket will take before it is useless to me.

I look around for anything I can use as a weapon. We are now on an open concrete pathway, no stones or loose gravel, nothing at all within arm's reach.

I turn my attention back to Mike, attempting to judge the angle of his next attack. He comes in low but moves high at the last moment, the knife held down by his thigh.

His bare hand is dangerous, but the blade is deadly.

He strikes with both simultaneously, his fist coming in for a neck blow while the knife goes low for a belly strike.

I stop them at the same time, one hand at his throat, the other catching the wrist of his knife arm.

He twists hard, bringing the blade up toward my chest. We are leaning in head-to-head, arm-to-arm, locked in the struggle. The blade inches closer to its target.

"You still have the scar, don't you?" he says. "Do you remember how you got it?"

I think back to graduation day, the final battle with Mike that ended with my being stabbed.

"I remember," I say. "And I remember that I graduated despite you."

I was hurt, but I was not defeated.

Mike says, "You think you stopped me from killing you that day."

"That's exactly what happened," I say.

"You're wrong."

Don't listen to him. This is another mind game. Defeat your opponent in the head, and you will defeat him in the world.

He says, "You thought I was trying to kill you, and you were strong enough to prevent it. You think that's the reason you graduated."

"I know why I graduated," I say.

Mike shakes his head. "Your father wouldn't risk my killing you. My job was to challenge you like you'd never been challenged before."

"You stuck a knife in my chest. If that's not trying to kill me, I don't know what is."

"You want to know why I stabbed you, Zach? I was making a hole. Those were my mission orders. Make a hole so your father could hide the chip inside you. That way you would never know about it."

Is it possible that the entire fight was staged to create the illusion that I had defeated Mike?

I release my grip on him. He smiles and steps back.

"I pulled my strike," he says. "I kept the blade from penetrating deeper. Do you remember in the clinic afterward, what Mother told you?"

I remember Mother showed me the CT scan. She told me I was two millimeters away from death. Just a little deeper and the blade would have nicked my aorta and I would have bled out.

Mike grins ear to ear. "Pretty good, huh?"

"Pretty good."

The grin disappears. He waves the knife in the air.

"I have different mission orders this time," he says. "You heard Mother. She told me to finish the job."

"Do your best," I say.

"With pleasure," he says.

I look at Mike preparing for his final attack, and a strange feeling comes over me. This is the boy I've hated, the one who took my old life from me, who let me think he had killed my father. This boy who was the source of so much of my suffering. I know I should hate him, but looking at him now, I just feel sorry for him.

I push the feeling away. There is no room for compassion in a fight. It is dangerous, even deadly.

I take a moment and steel my mind against him.

I am ready.

Mike rushes at me from across the yard, roaring as he comes.

He's six feet away. Then four.

He leaps.

The blade extends out as I see his attack form in the air in front of me.

I prepare to meet it—

Suddenly there is a loud clapping sound, and Mike stops two feet away from me and drops the knife.

His hand flies up to the side of his head. He holds it there, confusion forming on his face.

"What the hell?" he says.

A line of blood eases from between his fingers. He lowers his hand and looks at the blood.

That's when I see there's a hole in the side of his head.

A bullet hole.

He stumbles toward me, unsteady on his feet.

I step back quickly, prepared to defend myself, but there's no need. Mike falls to his knees in front of me, his eyes roll back into his head, and he collapses.

Only then do I see the exit wound, the back of his head blown out to expose the gray matter beneath.

I catch a glint of sunlight out of the corner of my eye.

I look up to the roof of a small building across the quad.

Tanya sits up, a rifle with a silencer in her hands. She waves to me.

Then she swings the rifle across one shoulder, scurries across the roof, slides down a drainpipe, and hops to the ground.

I watch her all the way until she sidles up next to me.

"Did you just kill Mike?" I say.

She glances down at his lifeless body.

"Looks that way," she says.

"Why?"

"He was an asshole."

Hard to disagree with her.

"Tanya, what about those things you said in the gym—"

"A performance for Mother. When they captured us at the baseball field, I knew I had to survive long enough to help you. If Mother thought I was still on my mission, I might get the chance."

I look down at Mike's body.

"You got the chance. That's for sure."

She steps back from the spreading pool of blood.

"I guess I broke protocol," she says.

"More than broke it. You've gone rogue."

"I went rogue a long time ago," she says.

"When?"

"I was pretty rogue in the bedroom, wasn't I?"

"I think I'm blushing," I say.

"I kind of like it," she says.

I look around the quad. The young Program recruits seem to have deserted the area. It's possible they are massing elsewhere, preparing to attack. I try to imagine what Mother's contingency plan might be in this situation.

I glance over at Tanya to ask her. I get distracted by the way the rifle strap cuts across her chest, pressing the fabric against her breasts.

"Eyes up, Zach. Are you looking at the gun or my chest?"

"To be honest, a little of both."

She grins. "How do you want to play this?" she says.

"Howard first. Then I'm going to find Mother."

She checks the safety on the rifle, then swings it down into a carry position.

"I think I know where they're keeping Howard," she says.

"Lead the way."

TANYA GUIDES ME INTO THE BASEMENT OF A NEARBY BUILDING.

She opens a heavy metal door to reveal a hidden tunnel.

"These run underground throughout the campus," she says. "We use them to get around in the winter."

"Anything to be concerned about?"

"You mean like booby traps?"

"That's a good start."

"Not that I know of. But I'll go first if it makes you feel better."

She starts down the tunnel before I can stop her, and I have to hurry to catch up. Tanya moves with purpose, zigzagging this way and that before pausing in front of a door marked with a painted number.

"I think this is the right building," she says.

We pop out into a different basement than the one we began in.

She says, "I tried to get myself assigned as his interrogator, but they wouldn't allow it, not without knowing exactly what happened in the field."

"It could be bad, that's what you're saying."

She nods.

"Just show me where he is," I say.

We walk around the corner, stopping at a door locked from the outside.

"In here," she says.

I go first this time, hurrying to undo the latch and pull the door open.

I'm staring into a cold concrete cell, a chair bolted to the floor in the center of the room.

Howard is strapped to it.

At the sound of the door, his head snaps up, his expression defiant. It takes him a moment to realize it's us.

"Holy crap," he says. "It's about time."

I run toward him, undoing the leather bands around his chest.

"Did they hurt you?" I ask.

"Mostly my pride," he says. He stretches, wincing in pain. "It looks like I'm the one in the torture chair this mission."

"You know what they say: It's not a real mission until someone's in a torture chair."

We both laugh.

"You two are nuts," Tanya says.

"Inside joke," Howard says.

I check his eyes and upper body. He's been roughed up quite a bit, but he doesn't appear to be gravely injured.

"I thought The Program was something cool," he says. "But these are not nice people you work with."

"I don't work with them anymore."

Tanya and I trade looks.

"What happened while I was locked up?" Howard says. "I heard alarms going off."

"It's a long story that will have to wait for later," I say. "Right now you need to know there's a whole campus of soldiers on alert above us. And Mother is leading them."

"What about Mike?" Howard says with a shiver.

"He's dead," I say.

"Good. He was an asshole."

"That's what Tanya said."

Tanya gives us a thumbs-up, then goes back to watching the hall.

Howard stands up, leaning on me to steady himself as I pat his arms and legs to restore blood flow.

"Did you find your father?" he says.

He must see something in my face, because he squeezes my shoulder.

I glance to the door. Tanya is watching and listening. I realize she doesn't know what happened, either.

"My father is gone," I say. "I'll tell you both about it later."

Tanya nods and redirects her attention out the door.

"All clear in the hallway," she says. "But it might not be that way for long."

"I'm going to get you guys out of here," I say, "and then I'll look for Mother."

"Mother could be long gone by now," Tanya says.

"I don't think so," I say.

"Why not?" Tanya says.

"Endgame. We haven't had ours yet."

"I'm not leaving without you," Howard says.

"Me, either," Tanya says. "We're in this together, remember?"

Both of them have determined expressions on their faces.

Howard shrugs. "Looks like you're stuck with us," he says.

"I guess there are worse people to be stuck with," I say.

They both smile.

"How will we find Mother?" Howard says.

"I'm pretty sure I know where she is," I say.

THIS USED TO BE MY HOME.

The farmhouse. I trained here for two years when I first arrived at The Program. It is the place where I ended one life and began a new one.

If I have my way, the same thing will happen again today.

The house is just as I remember it. A three-story, gray-planked structure with white lighting fixtures around the exterior. It looks deserted as we first approach, but as we walk up the front drive, young Program soldiers begin to appear from behind the house. They spread out around us with weapons drawn, sealing off any means of escape.

The front door opens, and Mother steps out. It looks like she's been waiting for me. I wonder if she knows Mike is dead, or if she knew all along that I would win that battle. I suppose it doesn't matter now.

She's dressed casually in a dark gray button-down sweater and the new glasses I saw her wearing earlier. If it weren't for the armed soldiers around us, you might think we'd been invited over for a dinner party.

"I'm going to talk to her," I say.

"We'll go together," Tanya says.

"Alone," I say.

"Do you want to take the gun?" Tanya asks, offering me her sniper rifle.

I look around at the two dozen young soldiers on all sides of us. They're on edge since Mother came out of the house, fingers inside trigger guards.

"I think you'd better put the gun on the ground, Tanya."

"I've got nine rounds left in the mag, and I don't miss."

"Nine won't get the job done," I say.

She takes the gun from her shoulder and gently places it on the ground.

I look at Mother on the front steps waiting for me. I start toward her.

Tanya reaches out and stops me with a touch.

"Do you know what you're doing, Zach?"

"No idea," I say. "But I've got a talent for improvisation."

"Oh crap," Howard says.

I wink at him, and I turn and walk toward Mother.

Several of the soldiers move to intercept me, but Mother motions them back with a wave of her hand.

I walk forward and stop at the bottom of the stairs.

"Welcome home," Mother says.

Memories of my training flash in my head. Physical combat, weapons strategy, tactical classes. Everything I am today was formed in this house.

Not everything. I was a boy before I was a soldier.

"You knew I'd come here," I say.

"I suspected as much," she says. "So I made sure we had an audience." She indicates the soldiers that surround us. "I want them to see this. I want them to understand."

"Understand what, Mother?"

"What it means to be a family."

"A family is supposed to support life. You've stolen these kids' lives, just like you stole mine. You and my father together."

"What were you before us?" Mother says. "Some kid in the suburbs, indistinguishable from thousands of others. You were a nobody. We made you somebody."

"You took away my identity."

"We gave you an identity, just as we gave identities to all the soldiers around you. That is your father's inspiration."

"He's dead," I say. "That inspiration died with him."

Mother speaks loudly now, making sure she can be heard by the crowd around us.

"You want to go back to living a normal life?" she says. "Let me tell you what it means to be normal. It's boring, purposeless. If you're lucky, you'll spend a fortune to go to college and maybe grad school, and what will you have to show for it? A diploma with your name on it and a job staring at Excel spreadsheets all day. Or, if you're brilliant and you beat the system, maybe you'll create an app, so people can play, killing zombies, forgetting for a second they've become zombies themselves. You'll get rich and join the one percent, and you'll fool yourself into thinking you've achieved something. But the truth is, you'll live and die and make no difference at all in the world, just like everyone else."

"I don't believe that," I say.

"You're sixteen years old. You have no idea of the life that awaits you out there. You don't know it, but you have everything you need in the world right now. You have purpose, you have a mission. That's irreplaceable."

"The mission is everything," I say. "Just like you taught me."

"That's right," Mother says. "Because without a mission, we are nothing. We are walking dead."

Mother comes closer, her voice low.

"I used to be one of those people," she says. "But no more. I'd rather die than go back there."

"That's your choice, not mine."

"You have a purpose now, Zach. We have a purpose together. If you walk away, you risk getting lost forever."

"I'm willing to take that risk," I say.

Mother sighs, the energy seeming to drain from her.

"I had so much hope for you," she says. "You were going to be the greatest soldier in the world."

She comes all the way down the stairs, standing face-to-face with me. Her voice is a whisper.

"You can still be great," she says.

"Mike is dead," I say. "Father, too. All because of me."

Her face does not register any emotion.

"I believe in survival of the fittest," Mother says. "The weak die. The strong survive. Perhaps it was meant to be you and me from the beginning, a mother and her son, leading them all."

Mother opens her arms. Her expression softens, her eyes focused on mine.

"Come, Zach. Let's make this right between us."

I step closer, drawn by the warmth in her voice. She smiles and brushes the hair from her forehead. For a moment I imagine what she might have been like when she was my age, a teenager dreaming of the future.

"Your father is dead," she says, "but you still have a family if you want one. You were right about Howard. We need him, and Tanya, too. All of us can rebuild together."

I am closer to her than I've ever been before. I can see individual pores in her skin, the mascara around her eyes, strands of gray starting to show in her sandy-blond hair.

"Call me a pragmatist," she says, "but I'm not willing to lose all we've worked for."

Mother puts a hand on my shoulder. She squeezes gently.

"I know your father didn't get to install your new chip," she says. "I imagine you must be having a lot of confusing feelings right now. Seeing the house again. And seeing me, Zachary."

Something softens inside when I hear Mother say my name.

I step into her arms and she hugs me, her body warm against mine. She holds me close and whispers to me, telling me everything is going to be okay. Mother's scent mingles with the memory of my father from years ago, the way he would hold me on his lap while he worked at his desk at home. I think of my real mother tucking me in at night, pulling the blanket up high until I felt the soft fabric against my chin. Then she'd lean over, put a hand on my chest, and kiss me on the forehead.

I used to have parents. I used to have a family.

Mother holds me tight with one arm. With the other she removes her glasses and wipes a tear from her eye.

She's crying.

"I'm sorry," she says. "I'm unexpectedly emotional."

"Me, too," I say.

"You're a good boy," she says. "I'm sorry about this mess we're in."

Something glints in the corner of my vision. Mother is holding the glasses by her side, twisting them in her fingers, the metal frames catching sunlight.

They fall out of her hand and hit the ground.

"I dropped my glasses," she says.

Her grip tightens on my shoulder as she leans on me for balance, stooping down to retrieve the glasses.

She comes up quickly. Too quickly.

My senses ramp up to high alert.

I am in danger.

By the time I realize it, my body is already in motion.

I grab hold of Mother's forearm, stopping it in midair. She has detached the temple piece from her glasses, and she's holding it tightly in her hand, the weaponized needle out and ready to strike.

The needle comes closer as Mother fights to get within striking distance.

"I'll do anything to save The Program," she says through gritted teeth. "If you're not with me, then you're a liability."

We struggle for a moment, the needle shifting back and forth between us. Mother is stronger than I imagined. But as strong as she is, I am stronger.

She makes one last effort to plunge the weapon into my flesh.

She fails.

I counter her movement, pulling her wrist across her body, and pushing the weapon through the cotton weave on the arm of her sweater, until the needle makes contact with her skin.

It pierces for a second and a half. No more.

Enough time for me to depress the plunger, for the poison that was meant for me to enter her body.

She drops the weapon. She looks at me, stunned. She falls to her knees, immediately fighting for breath.

The poison is fast. It moves at the speed of blood.

"Son," she says.

"I'm not your son. I never was."

Three seconds later Mother's eyes close and she collapses at my feet.

I lean down and check her pulse with two fingers on the side of her neck. The skin is still warm there, my touch strangely intimate.

I resist the impulse to pull away. I leave my fingers there until I am sure her heart is no longer beating. Only then do I stand up.

Mother is gone. And with her, the leadership of The Program.

I stretch and look toward the sky. It is a clear bright blue, unmarred by clouds.

I lean my head back and breathe deeply. I feel my lungs fill and release.

I am alive. I am free.

Almost.

Because the children of The Program are everywhere, their numbers having increased while Mother and I were talking. There are at least fifty of them now. Some watch from the doorway, others peer out from the windows of the farmhouse above me. The majority stand around the yard in a large circle.

Their faces tell a story. They are in shock.

I slowly back away from Mother's body. The soldiers' eyes follow me, as do their gun barrels.

I can imagine how it might play out. I would fight with Tanya by my side, and many of the soldiers would die, but not all. Their numbers are too great, and eventually they would overpower us.

I move in close to Tanya and Howard, the three of us staring at the soldiers, who stare back at us.

"This is bad," Howard says under his breath.

"Stay calm," I say.

"We can't take them all on," Tanya says.

She's thinking the same thing I was. But I can't give in to negativity. Attitude is everything in a fight.

"We'll take them out one at a time," I say. "Stick together. Fight for as long as you can."

Tanya glances at me. I see the doubt on her face, but she's putting up a brave front. Maybe for Howard. Maybe for the both of us.

One of the older boys steps out from among the soldiers. He is perhaps fourteen years old, still lanky in his movements, but I can sense that he is well on his way to being an assassin.

The boy looks back at Mother's body on the ground.

"You killed her," he says.

"I did," I say.

"And I heard you say that Dr. Abram is dead, too."

"Yes."

I prepare for him to strike, but he does not.

"What are we supposed to do now?" he says.

The question confuses me. I look at the young soldiers around us. They lean in, listening, faces curious.

Is it possible they're not going to fight?

"You're free." I say it loudly so I can be heard around the yard. "All of you."

"Free to what?" the boy asks.

"Free to go."

"Our real parents are dead. Where are we supposed to go?"

Howard puts a hand on my arm, urging me to look to the right. The kids are coming forward, forming up beside us.

I look out at the faces of the assassins-in-training. They are a part of The Program, but not all of it. There are dozens of child hackers spread out in a network across the country, secretly embedded in society.

I start to formulate a plan for dismantling The Program.

Maybe Howard can send a message to the hackers, dissolving the network and instructing them to reintegrate into the real world. They might be able to do so without anyone knowing.

What about the soldiers around me?

I could call the authorities and tell them the story of a military-training facility gone awry, spun into treasonous acts by an insane commander. But what credibility will I have now that I've been labeled a terrorist?

And what would happen to these kids, their families missing or murdered by The Program? Will they be treated like children or terrorists?

Maybe they can be adopted and find new lives, new families, new hope for the future.

Or maybe they will be pariahs, lost in a society that will forever brand them as child killers.

I glance up to find a small, blond-haired girl looking at me. She is maybe eight years old, the toughness in her eyes undermined by a trembling lip below. She's trying her best not to cry.

She gathers the courage to come forward, craning her neck as she looks up at me.

"Tell us what to do," she says.

I look at the faces around me.

They are children. They are soldiers.

And now they are homeless.

Tanya pushes in closer to me.

"We're all they have," she whispers.

"It's true," Howard says.

The Program no longer exists, but someone has to take responsibility for these soldiers. Maybe there is a new mission for them. A mission with a different purpose.

For that to happen, someone has to pick up the torch and carry it in a different direction.

My mind is whirling.

"What now?" Tanya says.

I look at her and Howard standing with me. I gaze at the soldiers waiting in front of us.

I make my decision.

"Is there a cafeteria around here?" I ask Tanya.

"On campus." She indicates one of the buildings in the area we left a short time ago.

I raise my voice so the soldiers can hear me.

"Is anyone hungry?" I ask them.

Heads nod down the line.

Howard smiles. Tanya reaches over and takes my hand.

"Follow me," I say to the soldiers.

And they do.

ACKNOWLEDGMENTS

It's been a long and wonderful journey bringing this trilogy into the world. I haven't done it alone.

It began with my agent Stuart Krichevsky, who believed before anyone else and did what he does best. Many thanks to him, Ross Harris, and Shana Cohen at SKLA. They've been with me every step of the way, and I can't thank them enough.

Thanks to my editor Kate Sullivan and publisher Megan Tingley, who championed the series and invited me into the LBYR family. I will be forever grateful to them and to the team at LBYR, past and present, who have supported the books: Andrew Smith, Lisa Moraleda, Melanie Chang, Victoria Stapleton, Leslie Shumate, Faye Bi, Jenny Choy, Amy Habayeb, Kristin Dulaney, and many more.

Very special thanks to my editor Pam Garfinkel, who swooped in like an action hero to save the day on Book 3. She even made it look easy.

Thanks to the good folks at Orchard UK and the many international partners who have brought the series to readers around the world.

I want to give a special shout-out to Lauren Fischer and Rich Tackenberg, best friends who have cheered me from the sidelines, read my books, listened to my hopes and fears, and refilled my coffee cup on Saturday mornings. I couldn't have done it without them.

Finally, I'd like to thank the readers, bloggers, teachers, librarians, and booksellers who have read and shared the books. If you're reading this now, you've likely followed the assassin's journey from the very beginning. Bravo to you.

And now, my friends, it's time for me to get back to writing.

Douglas Hill

ALLEN ZADOFF

is the author of several acclaimed
novels, including *I Am the Mission;
I Am the Weapon*, a Top Ten Quick
Pick for Reluctant Young Adult
Readers; and *Food, Girls, and Other
Things I Can't Have*, winner of the Sid
Fleischman Humor Award and a YALSA
Popular Paperback for Young Adults.
He is a graduate of Cornell University
and the Harvard University Institute
for Advanced Theater Training. His
training as a super spy, however, has
yet to be verified.

**ALLEN INVITES YOU TO VISIT HIM AT
THEUNKNOWNASSASSIN.COM.**